FINISHING SCHOOL

G.D.Grey
(Editor)

Also by G.D. Grey

Nursery School – Ebook and in Paperback

G.D.Grey (Editor)

FOREWORD

The following events have been pieced together by the editor from the diaries and daybooks of the persons to which they are attributed and have been edited by the various authors at a much later date than their original. Every effort has been made to ensure the authenticity of the accounts, but the very exercise of some of the revisions may have engendered the occasional anachronism. Some of the accounts, particularly those of the Matron and the Headmistress were obtained under the Freedom of Information Act, which has enabled the editor to access these accounts which were originally submitted to the investigating authority by the officer in charge of the events first chronicled in Chapters VII.

G.D. Grey – Editor

CHAPTER 1

Alice

"Finishing school?" I asked in astonishment. "You are joking, surely: I really cannot believe that you just said that."

I turned to look at Rachel who was seated beside me at our kitchen table. Our parents were dotted round the table facing us. My mother Vera, stocky, black-haired and feisty, glared back at me. Tom, my father, lean and bronzed, a very fit and athletic figure seemingly preoccupied with something invisible on the table in front of him and Rachel's parents, Joseph and Rebecca, almost the archetypical Jewish couple looking at us with kindly sympathy at the same time hugging a little secret joke together. Rachel said nothing.

"Do you seriously think that we want to spend one minute of our time farting about learning how to curtsey and make ourselves desirable properties so that we can become some businessman's wanking machine?"

My father raised his head and looked me straight in the eye.

"You do have such an expressive way of putting things, my darling," he murmured pleasantly. My mother snorted. Jerry, my father's brother who made up those present, chuckled. "No laughing matter," snapped my mother. "We are trying to find the right avenue for your further education, so it would be a good idea if you didn't adopt this flippant attitude."

"Well, I for one don't want some moneyed prat walking up my right avenue thank you very much!" I declared.

"I don't think that's really very likely, do you?" my father replied. "After all, any male wanting that sort of wife would run a mile from either of you. Not," he hastened to add, "that you are not both very attractive and eminently desirable, but neither of you are complaisant or biddable. In any case, the finishing we have in mind for you both is rather more than the mere acquisition of etiquette, deportment and social graces."

Rachel's parents were now both grinning openly and Jerry gave a shout of laughter. "Told you," he chortled. My mother was still scowling. "Where she picks up such language is beyond me," she declared. "Anybody would think we lived in the gutter."

"Give over, ducks," Jerry said. "You know that would have been your reaction too."

"So how does this school differ in it its finishing process?" Rachel asked, "from other finishing schools, that is. Surely that is the whole purpose of a finishing school; to train young females for the marriage market, so that they can be sold off like cattle to the wealthy and well connected."

"There is an element of choice, you know" Joseph put in. "You're not obliged to marry anybody you don't like. It's just an education for living in high society."

"But marriage is the ultimate goal all the same, isn't it."

"Sometimes, I agree, but that's something that many people desire at all levels of society."

"We're getting off the point here," my mother brought her fist down on the table. "This school has more to offer than a marriage bureau."

"Of course it does," agreed my father. "Let me explain a bit more about this institution. It is a genuine finishing school for women and there are students there solely for that purpose who want a career in business as well as marriage, but there is a secondary stream of tuition which is virtually up to university standard. Alice, you will find yourself advancing in your language studies at an amazing rate as will you, Rachel, with your scientific interests so there's no need to think that we have given up on you and are just throwing you onto the marriage market."

"Never let it be said that we don't understand you," Jerry remarked - rather snidely, I thought. I looked at him coldly. Uncle or not I did not think he had any right to comment on our relationship. I was actually very fond of him, we all were, but he did have a sardonic streak in him that could be rather upsetting at times. His resemblance to his brother was uncanny; people were often confusing the two of them especially, when as sometimes happened, he was minding the family garden store in the village. Joseph and Rebecca both gave him a reproachful look and my mother positively glared.

"Enough!" she said. "There is a third line of education which will be made available to you if you go there and also if you are deemed adequate enough. You won't be told any more about this until your interview, so don't think that it is just up to you whether you go there or not. Neither of you wish to go to University so this is the next best thing if you are to make something of your abilities. You are both of an age when it is essential you make up your minds to grow up."

Looking at Rachel I saw that she was as taken aback as I was at the vehemence in my mother's words.

"Just go for the interview and then you'll both see the place and get the feel of it. I guarantee you will find it attractive.," my father said.

"It's true," Jerry added. "You will probably take to it like ducks to water and apologies for snide remark."

"The headmistress is a very remarkable woman," Rebecca said. "She is very striking in many ways and is extremely intelligent. I think you will like each other very well. Also, please do consider us as well. We four are going to be out of the country for some considerable time and going to some very hostile environments. We want you to be safe and well looked after, which is also one of the reasons we are recommending this school to you."

"You know that we have every faith in you," Joseph added, "and that you are both very capable as well as very mature for your age, but at the same time it would ease our minds if we knew that you were in safe hands. We can't come back at a moment's notice from wherever we are, because nobody will know wherever we are, do you see?" The poor man was almost in tears: it would have been a stony heart that could resist that plea.

"Here's the prospectus, madam," my mother handed over the shiny brochure. "You just have a look at that and see whether it meets with your approval!" My mother could be very trying at times. I pushed it towards Rachel so that we could both have a squint at it.

"Nice looking house," she commented. "Is this a walled garden?"

"It's actually a walled village," my father said. "One of the few remaining in this part of the world, and it's quite a magnificent old house, recently converted. The school was started by Yvette Coleman some thirty years ago, got taken over by the M.O.D. for a short spell, then bought and refurbished by His Highness Prince Salim who came into a little bit of pocket money when an oil well was sunk at the bottom of his garden, figuratively speaking. In fact his father was the first recipient of this windfall, but he died shortly after the money started to flow in. This is his son who inherited it: he was being thoroughly westernised at Oxford when his father died. Consequently he introduced all sorts of things naturally detested by the hardline clerics of the day, such as democracy, equal rights for women and all citizens, education, repeal of Sharia law or at least some of its more repellent aspects. So he is not very popular in certain circles although his own people love him and attribute their success and happiness to his liberalisation."

"Who wrote this appalling bumf on the front page?" I demanded. "Listen; *The Yvette Coleman Finishing School for Young Ladies occupies a good-sized former family mansion situated within the confines of the walled village of Silverton which is itself situate on the northern edge, yet contained within, the boundaries of Dartmoor National Park.* It sounds just like some crappy estate agent wrote it when he was pissed."

"Not the finest prose, I admit," my father replied urbanely, "but it helps to keep unwanted attention away from the place. All part of the discretion necessary to hide it deepest secrets."

Rachel and I glanced at each other. Underneath the light-hearted banter there was the usual element of truth that my parents conveyed. It was never discussed openly but it was evident that both our parents were sometimes caught up in some rather disturbing events on their trips abroad. Until now one set of parents had always remained at home to look after the two of us.

"When shall we be going for our interview?" Rachel asked.

"How about tomorrow!" said my mother. "We've fixed it up anyway, so we could well have done without all these histrionics." She glared at me, stood up and swept out of the kitchen.

"Term starts next month, so you will have time to work out what you want to concentrate on when you've had a chat with the Head. She's very helpful. You'll be surprised," my father said.

It was a pleasant evening, so Rachel and I poured ourselves some home-made lemonade and went out and sat in the garden. There was a two-seater garden swing in the shade of an ancient apple tree which we found very restful on occasion. I sometimes think that the evening light shows Rachel up at her best. She has the sort of features and build favoured by the pre-Raphaelites, a sort of golden earthy quality that was quite robust and solidly tangible. Perhaps I'm being somewhat tautological here, but I always think one can't have too much of a good thing.

"You're thinking about me aren't you," she said. "Am I covered in smuts or have I broken out in some sort of rash, mayhap?"

"You really do talk crap sometimes," I said pleasantly. "No, you idiot. I was just thinking how completely Burne Jones you are, like one of his lush warm raven-haired beauties and how much I love you."

"Sweetheart, come sit beside me and I shall shower you with kisses and tell you how much I adore you in return. Also," she said, patting the seat invitingly beside her, "you are like a pre-Raphaelite Madonna, and far too beautiful altogether for you own good."

I seated myself beside her, "I suppose perfection does become somewhat trying after a time, doesn't it," I said smugly. I leant against her comfortingly. "Do you want to do this finishing school thing?" I asked her. "Really?"

"It will probably be quite a lot of fun, you know," Rachel said dreamily. "It's high time we got out a bit more. Do you realise we've never really been anywhere else but here all our lives? Most kids of our age have been round the world at least once."

"Like to New Zealand for a couple of months and then maybe a stop off at Hong Kong on the way back?" I scoffed. "Hardly foreign travel."

"You're thinking of Daisy and her sister with a cousin in Auckland. There are other places and other kids of our age."

"Do you realise we'll both be eighteen by the time we start at this place?" I know I sounded a bit querulous, but I was fretful about everything that day. Too many unknowns seemed to be hanging over us; the idea of living as boarders in a completely different environment from our lovely independent school with its amazing Headmistress where we had spent the last few years of our lives and we had been so happy. Not that we had all those many close friends as we had been so dependent on each other over the years which was not surprising really. Our respective mothers had met at the pre-natal clinic and had taken to each other as only diametrical opposites sometimes can. My mother, all nervous energy and irascibility and Rebecca, coolness and loving tenderness. Our fathers seemed more compatible on first impressions but there was a huge difference in their basic temperaments. Joseph is, like his wife, a totally compassionate human being. My father, on the hand, is a very cool customer.

I realised suddenly that I was on the verge of tears. I understood that it was fundamentally due to hormonal changes in my still pubescent body, but that didn't stop the misery. It became more and more unbearable and Rachel, seeing the expression on my face, put a comforting arm round my shoulders. That did it of course. Next moment I was sobbing my heart out.

"I don't want to go away," I wailed. "I want to stay here with you and Mum and Dad and Rebecca and Joseph and the dogs and the ponies and live here for ever. I love this place and everybody in it. Why do I have to leave it?"

The tears were pouring down my face by now. Rachel hugged me to her and stroked my tear-sodden face. "It's all going to be destroyed and I'll never see anybody again and we'll be in some god-awful dump of an institution, and.....and...."

"Listen, sweetheart," Rachel murmured in my ear, "we'll be all right you know. We have each other and we'll have fun and learn lots of things and make heaps of new and lovely friends and everybody will adore us then we'll come home and our parents will be so proud of us and they will tell us all their adventures and we'll have a huge party with Anna and Timmy, Harold and Frank and all the local boys and girls. We might even invite the vicar - he's quite fun is Fanny Adams."

And so she soothed me and put my mind to rest and we had an early night together and awoke all refreshed first thing the next morning. I've learnt to accept these weird crying fits. Rachel has her moments too, but in her case, she goes somewhere far away in her mind and just for a few moments there's nobody there. Bloody hormones!

* * *

The following day my father drove us over to the school which was only a few miles away from our homes. It had been decided that one parent was quite enough of an imposition for this visit. My mother would probably have been counter-productive and Rachel's parents had a conference to go to. If it worked out that we went to the school, and I honestly couldn't see that, as far as we were concerned, there was all that much choice in the matter, then we would go there as boarders and might even have to remain there during holiday periods if necessity arose. The headmistress, Lucy Davison, explained that a skeleton staff were kept on at all times as there was much to do in the general running of the place which needed attending to; not least of which were the stables and string of ten horses and a number of farm animals, all of whom had to be catered for at all times.

"We could hardly send the horses off to the seaside for a holiday, and heaven alone knows who would give bed and board to the other animals," she said as she shepherded us round the building. "Especially the pigs," she added, "such fussy eaters! Now here," she threw open a door at the end of a long corridor on the upper story of the house, "would be your room if you join us for the following term."

"Here" was a long, rather narrow room running at right angles to the corridor. At the end of the room was a large framed mirror which covered the whole of the back wall. Behind the door stood a single bed; another bed stood on the lengthwise wall opposite the window area. There were two windows which looked out over an apple orchard and what appeared to be a vegetable garden behind that. It was a delightful view. Two writing desks had been placed directly underneath the windows and the room was pleasantly carpeted and furnished with a couple of comfortable looking office chairs at the desks. There was also a small sink and wall sockets at floor level.

"There used to be a wall-length mirror facing the window as this was used as a ballet practice room," she explained. "We changed the curriculum quite drastically some years ago and unfortunately ballet had to go. It really is not much use having it as a part-time subject and there are enough special schools in that field anyway."

"Was that something you were keen on?" Rachel asked her. I think she had also detected a shade of wistfulness in the headmistress's voice. She smiled, "Some girls go pony mad; I was ballet mad." Lucy Davison was probably about forty years old, I decided, and a very striking lady indeed. She had that perfect creamy complexion that is either completely natural or comes at great cost accompanied by a whole cartload of pretension and personal conceit. So far there had not been the slightest signs of any of these undesirable qualities. I realised that I was beginning to like the idea of coming here.

"What about the other boarders?" I asked her. "Do they all have their own rooms?"

"It's a mixture," she replied. "There are some dormitories which sleep six or eight girls, a few single rooms and a couple of other double rooms. We try and accommodate the boarders according to their needs. As the pair of you are used to being with each other I thought it sensible to give you this as first choice. If you would prefer another arrangement, I'm sure it could be organised."

"No, really," Rachel laughed. "This will be lovely for us - that is," she added, "if you accept us as students." The headmistress smiled at her. "How very modest," she said approvingly. "If you are willing, we would like to give you a short written test to assess your literacy and mathematical standard which you can take today if, of course, you are happy to stay a little longer?" she looked at my father for confirmation. "Of course, we are in no hurry and it would be good to get it sorted out today in any case," he agreed.

"Excellent," she said. "If you would care to stay to lunch we can provide you with our standard holiday fare. Basics really, but we grow most of our produce on the estate and also supply much of the meat and dairy for our students and staff, so we know the quality. But I believe Alice and Rachel are vegetarians and we cater for them as well as carnivores."

This was even better news. I could feel that Rachel was completely won over by the attractive Lucy Davison and I had forgotten about last night's tantrum and was getting quite excited about the idea of coming here. Our own bedroom - Wow! Lucy Davison certainly knew how to make a couple of girls very happy.

We stopped on the way back to the main hall and refectory so that Rachel and I could fill in the test paper which we had each been given. We noticed that they were completely different with the exception of the final requirement which was to write a short essay on any subject we chose. I wrote an account of the Cavalier poets, some of whom I had come across recently and found very attractive; Rachel wrote a short monologue on the chemical analysis of blood groups and its history.

It was getting on for lunch time and we found our way to the refectory where my father stood chatting to the headmistress and a dark-skinned, good looking man in his mid-thirties. An imposing but pleasant looking lady, who was of what my parents would have termed an uncertain age, made up the group

The head beckoned us over and introduced us to His Highness Prince Salim, Patron of the school and Mrs. Penelope Broadchurch the Assistant Headmistress. Her husband, Peter, we later discovered, was the school's bursar.

We shook hands politely and gave our papers to Miss Davison. She glanced through them quickly and handed them over to her assistant. "Let's eat, shall we?" She led the way to the large table in the middle of the hall which had exactly six places already set. Either the staff where telepathic or she was a very clever organiser - or indeed, maybe both.

Conversation flowed easily under her calm air as hostess of the occasion. The prince proved to be an excellent conversationalist as did Mrs. Broadchurch. My father, as ever, was laconic but did contribute the *bon mot* from time to time. It was a very pleasant meal and at the end of it the headmistress, having interpreted some telepathic intelligence from both the assistant head and the patron, told us that we had both been accepted for enrolment in a month's time for the start of the new academic year.

"We do, however, want you to take the first part of our curriculum, that pertaining to etiquette, deportment and other social skills. We insist on that for any student who is taking advanced studies," she explained.

She held up a hand. "I know that this may seem arbitrary and indeed rather in the nature of an insult to people of your undoubted intelligence and ambitions, but I can assure you that in the event of you being invited on to our further advanced area of training, you will find it of inestimable value."

"What exactly is this third course of training?" I asked. "It really seems to be a bit of a mystery. Will we have to take the Official Secrets Act even if we decide to take it?"

The headmistress gave me a very straight look. "That would happen only if you decided not to take the course," she said. "Coo!" Rachel said, under her breath. We both chuckled.

"Cross that bridge when you come to it," advised my father. Of course he must have known what all this was about, but I knew that it would be like getting blood out of the proverbial to get him to divulge anything he was not of a mind to divulge.

"That's that, then," said the prince. "I'm sure you will have a great time here. I hope it doesn't sound too boastful, but this is really a most excellent seat of learning. We have subjects in our curriculum that are not taught in any other school in the world! Can you believe that?" He smiled expansively at us and I must confess to feeling somewhat overwhelmed by his enthusiasm and charm. The entire meal, in fact, had been one most successful sell and we were both totally hooked, and he knew it. We said good-byes to our hosts and drove home quite elated if we were truthful. My father is never one to say "I told you so!" and he didn't, but then, he didn't need to. My mother was in the garden when we got back. "All set, then?" she enquired. Dad just raised his eyebrows at her and she went and put the kettle on.

INTERLUDE

Tom

The decision to enrol our two girls in this institution was taken only after much thought and consideration by ourselves and our bosses in the Service. Vera, myself, Rebecca and Joseph were employed by government agencies to keep an eye on and report conditions from various hotspots around the globe. To that end our professional standing as botanists (Vera and myself), and medical researchers (Rebecca and Joseph), were useful cover for our clandestine observations. It took us to some of the remotest parts of the globe and naturally some of the most dangerous. Until that time it had been agreed that neither family would leave for an assignment unless the other family remained to care for the children. This had worked very well until earlier this year when our immediate superiors had been replaced with fresh young blood. Well, that was what was being bruited abroad. New Brooms. A Clean Sweep. Why such action should ever have been sanctioned was obscure. The unpalatable truth was that the new brooms were more in the nature of old toilet brushes that had been shoved down far too many lavatory pans! Consequently both our families had been ordered abroad for nine month stretches at the same time. All four of us handed in our resignations to take effect immediately; but we were persuaded to accept the commissions owing to the urgency of both operations, the unavailability of any replacements, and the promise of superior residential education for our girls alongside a substantially improved financial compensation all round. The reasons we agreed to the girls attending the school were twofold. They would be well looked after and they would be given a capital education which was unavailable anywhere else except at one of the major universities. The versatility of the school was striking. A student could take the finishing school prospectus and at the end of that year would be well equipped to be offered a prestigious post with an international firm, or a hand in marriage to a wealthy man, the choice was hers to make. Alternatively she could acquire a university entrance standard in a number of subjects ranging from mathematics to languages, history, science (bio and forensic), politics, economy, banking, classics and quantum physics taught by the best teachers anywhere. The third option, which was an add-on to either of the former courses, consisted of martial arts, weapons training, field-craft, spy-craft and allied clandestine pursuits. Friends of ours from the department had strongly suggested that whether or not we went abroad, this would suit both our girls admirably. They would relish the knowledge they would acquire because they were both highly intelligent; and they would also enjoy all the physical aspects of martial arts and they would be meeting many people of like intelligence and be in their element. They had the potential, so we were assured, to become first class agents in the field. An added inducement was that all the costs would be paid by the government; no strings would be attached to their acceptance or non-acceptance of the agency training, nor were the girls at any time committed to the life of a government agent unless they so wished. Only then did we agree to go, thinking that we had made a pretty good deal all round. I thought that once Alice and Rachel had met the Head and seen the school they would both be vey excited by the prospect of taking up residency. I was also sure that the prospect of martial arts training and playing with lethal weaponry would be like cream is to the cat.

I had already met with the headmistress a week before taking the girls over to Silverton. She was a charming lady whom I thought both girls would find very *simpatico* as I was pretty sure she was bi-sexual and assuredly broad-minded. This notion was reinforced when I explained how close our daughters were and how they were joined at the hip, metaphorically speaking.

"If they decide to enroll," she told me in her slightly husky voice, "I could offer them a delightful two-bedded room on the top floor. It's very spacious and they would be quite secluded there for their studies and also for their comfort. It had once been a ballet rehearsal room before the renovations a few years ago, and there still is an enormous mirror covering the end wall. Girls do so like a mirror, don't they?" I was somewhat at a loss to answer this but I must say that I found it a mildly suggestive remark. However I smiled noncommittally while she took me up to the top floor to show me the accommodation.

"They'll love it," I said enthusiastically. "All I have to do really is to bring them over to meet you and see whether you think they would be suitable students."

"From what you and others have told me about them I think they would be admirable. No doubt they will balk at the etiquette instruction but if they wish to take the auxiliary programme they will have to do a mini version of it, the reason for which I will explain when the time is right. Meanwhile, shall we make a date for bringing them over to meet me and possibly His Highness will be available that day and one or two of my senior colleagues." And so it had been arranged.

CHAPTER I (CONTD)

Alice

Almost a month to the day in mid-September found us back at the school and settling into our new home. We had limited ourselves to one large suitcase each which contained a couple of evening dresses with one extra special garment each for a grand occasion, a variety of tracksuits, jodhpurs for horse-riding, casual tops and bottoms, underwear and all the other paraphernalia of teenage girls and some little discreet extras which we kept well hidden away. Satisfied at last that we had everything where we wanted it we made our way down to the refectory as it was time for high tea. The prince, headmistress, assistant head and husband were already seated at the top of the large centre table and we were invited to join them. Not many pupils or staff had arrived yet as the term didn't start until the following Monday. It was mostly newcomers, students like ourselves who needed a bit of time to settle in, or those whose parents were not able to deliver their charges on a Monday. Seated across the table from us was a large, bouncy, freckle-faced girl of about our age, who quizzed us about our backgrounds while giving us the lowdown on the running of the school, teachers, other pupils and Things to Look Out For. All very entertaining and good practice for us in giving seemingly innocent, but factually evasive, answers. She introduced herself as Charlie, (real name Charlotte, but who wants to be called a pudding, what? Giggle, Splutter) "Indeed" we agreed courteously. "Wait 'til you meet the Fab Five though," she chortled. "They're really A-mazing, B-mazing and C-mazing!" We probably disappointed her in not enquiring further about the amazing qualities of her heroines, and by then we had reached the end of the meal and everybody seemed to be drifting out of the refectory towards the main hall. Lucy Davison indicated that we should go with her and she explained that although we would have a small enough audience, it should be enough for us. We regarded her with puzzlement - naturally!

"Newly enrolled students are encouraged to give a little talk as a way of introducing themselves to the staff and pupils. It is also good practice for when you are presented to those of a higher station in society than yourselves. And there is always someone," she added, amused at our reactions, "who is higher on the social scale than oneself in this best of all democracies."

What cynicism, I thought, from such charming lips. I grinned. "Well, we'll do our best," I assured her, "but unaccustomed as we are..."

She laughed. "Come along then, you will both sit up on the platform with us toffs. There are five other new girls this term who are here for the primary part of our system, so I think we'll put you two last if you don't mind."

The five she mentioned were in something of a state of tangled nerves and behaved like Miss World contestants whose passions were centred on babies and little fluffy kittens. Only one of them mentioned, in passing, that she enjoyed swimming, travelling and history. She was a determined looking girl with red hair and something of a truculent expression. I was puzzled as to the reason for her being here. Her name was Gloria and we would see something of her later.

Then I was up and talked reasonably well about my love of languages. I also inserted a couple of mildly racy stories which seemed to amuse some of the audience but bewilder the rest. Ah well, win some, lose some. Rachel rounded off the evening with a brilliant impromptu speech which had them rolling in the aisles. She has such a gift for public speaking that I think she could have made a good living out of being a professional after-dinner speaker. We were both congratulated and finally were free for night-time cocoa - can you believe it?

At last we were alone together. We had a sink and running water in our room which was quite a luxury and just had a rub-down in front of the sink. Toilets and bathrooms were at the other end of the corridor leading to our room so we had to pass quite a few of the other girls who were racing to get to the bathrooms first.

"Is this the usual night-time scrimmage, do you think?" asked Rachel. She gave me a searching look. "Oh, dear, you really are tired, aren't you!" She gave me a hug. "Do you just want to go straight to sleep?" I knew what she meant and smiled at her. "Just let me do my teeth and I promise to stay awake as long as possible."

"Don't force yourself," she said.

"No, and don't you force me either." We both giggled. I brushed my teeth and then fetched the hairbrush from my dressing table. Rachel sat on her dressing table chair facing the mirror and I started to brush her hair in long sweeping movements. Rachel had the loveliest hair, a rich dark brown with tiny hints of a deep red, almost scarlet light. This was quite an evening ritual we had developed over the years. We took it in turns to brush each others hair at night and that almost always resulted in one huge turn-on - either that or we fell asleep during the process and woke up in each others arms either later that night or in the morning.

"We'll have to be quiet, you know," she murmured drowsily. "We don't know how near anybody else is."

Some time later I remarked, "You know, I think we should have locked the door if we are going to get any sleep tonight. This bed is lovely but I think I need to go to my own." Rachel made no answer; she was fast asleep. I carefully disentangled myself and adjusting as much of her nightgown as I could and drawing the bedclothes over her, I locked the door and fell into my somewhat cold bed. How nice it would be, I thought, to have our lovely double bed here. I wonder of they would mind if we sent for it, and with that I fell fast asleep.

CHAPTER II

Rachel

I awoke the following morning to find Alice kneeling beside my bed and gazing into my freshly opened eyes. She leant over and kissed me softly and lingeringly on the lips.

One thing I have to say about Alice; she does give good orgasms. I was about to reach for her but she stood up suddenly saying that it was already after nine o'clock and we had better get a move on and be washed and dressed and in our right minds pretty sharpish or we would miss breakfast. I thought it probably finished by ten o'clock at the weekends, but I couldn't remember. Better safe than sorry, a girl needs her vittles of a morning. We made it in time before the porridge had started congealing - nothing worse than congealed porridge - well, yes, so many things are, I know. All the pupils were down with one or two exceptions but none of the older students seemed at all embarrassed by being late. (A good sign of tolerance, I thought). There was no sign of any of the staff apart from the Assistant Headmistress who was quietly buttering her toast when I looked across at her. She gave me a friendly smile and returned to the newspaper she had been reading. The girls were fairly subdued and there was no sign of the Fabulous Five, but I expected that they would only turn up at the very last minute. Alice and I found a couple of places at the other end of the table. The freckled airhead beamed at us from the other side of the table.

"Jolly good chatters last night, Ali," She caught my eye. "Yours was jolly good too, Rache - Super! Gosh, when I had to do it, I just sort of froze and went all sweaty, you know what I mean, but you were ever so cool."

I had a momentary vision of Charlie, (Charlotte, but Charlie to her friends), all sweaty and hot in a very compromising position with lots of jolly girls in similar positions lying in a tangle of limbs on a very plush bedspread and playing with all sorts of sex toys. Really, my mind sometimes! I glanced at Alice. She gave a little tight-lipped smile, so I imagined something similar had occurred to her. Honestly, the pair of us! I despair! I also thought I might ask her whether she had had similar thoughts when I had an opportunity. At that moment, Charlie got up to go and help herself from the tea-urn.

We turned to each other.

"Rache, were you thinking —?"

"Ali, were you thin——?"

Our thought processes were obviously still in tune with each other. The meal progressed. Miss Broadbent, having finished her coffee, stood up.

"Today," she said "You will be receiving your schedule of work for the term. The new girls will also be allocated their places in the various classes covering the subjects in which they are specialising together with schedules of the other subjects which they are expected to attend. Unless there are any sensible reasons for not attending these subjects they are mandatory. Alice and Rachel, please come and see me in my room when you have finished your breakfasts. One of the girls will direct you."

She left the refectory and the usual chatter broke out again.

"It's ever so easy" said Charlie, who had appointed herself our guide for the time-being. "I'll show you in a min."

We finished our breakfasts soon after and Charlie took us a mini-tour of the ground floor. "Classrooms, toilets, big hall which you've seen, entrance hall where you came in and gymnasium." She grinned. "Not only P.E. but self-defense," she explained. "Weapons training for the more advanced. Karate, aikido, that sort of thing is in the gym in the basement. Show you later."

"Weapons training?" asked Alice, a bit puzzled.

"Well, only sticks and fencing and things like that I mean, not rifles and machine-guns, whatever!"

"Ah!" We both breathed simultaneously.

* * *

"Now, girls," Miss Broadbent was seated on an upright chair at a small table in the window-bay of her pleasant room overlooking the orchard which appeared to be in full working order.

"You, Alice are taking Literature and languages so you will be in Shelley Class and you Rachel, being a science graduate in preparation will be appropriately in Marie Curie Class. We don't have school houses as you may know, because with the exception of some of the younger girls, most of you are now concentrating on your chosen subjects. Now, the extra-curricular subjects are for your personal development. We have such subjects as Etiquette, Deportment, Dancing, Equestrianism, History & Politics, what we call 'How-to', which covers the ability to speak in public, be interviewed for a position, interview others and converse with anybody from the milkman to royalty without turning a hair or feeling any embarrassment. Although you may eventually be taking specialist courses -" (here she bestowed a rather severe look on us as if to question the veracity of our choices), " - you will first be required to attend these principal studies for a certain period of time. The length of this part of your training will depend on how well you attend to these lessons."

She paused and looked at us expectantly.

"Are you saying," Alice asked, "that we are obliged to take Etiquette, Deportment and how to talk to the servants as serious subjects before we can proceed with our real disciplines?"

"Precisely so," Miss Broadbent said firmly. "Allow me to explain. You have chosen to take not only the secondary subjects, but also the possibility of the more advanced studies that this school has to offer. If you had chosen merely to pursue an academic or scientific career, there would be not much point in wasting your time on subjects the object of which is principally to get you a either a well paid position or a well heeled bedmate. Also the likelihood of the advanced course necessitates, strangely enough, the very virtues of that same category of training. You will on occasion find yourselves faced with being present at a diplomatic party or similar occasion, in which case you will have to know how to be at ease with people from all corners of the earth and of all customs. Do you know how to greet and converse with a Nigerian envoy, perhaps? Or an Albanian warlord? Or even a French Ambassador? The latter can be very tricky if you are not au *courant* with the latest Gallic fashion parade!" We contemplated this in silence.

"And how are you going to cope with riding to hound with the British gentry folk? They'll certainly see through you in a trice. No, if you are to be truly successful at your chosen careers, you must be competent in as many areas as is humanly possible. This is no course for the weak or undedicated person. So make your minds up now as to what you want to do with your lives. You both come recommended and encouraged by your parents and from one or two independent sources, but the final say is with you. If you decide to take the secondary path of education which is on offer, that will be fine. Also, I suppose," she looked a little depressed, "you could even go in for the primary and be satisfied with etiquette, deportment and dancing to get yourselves a rich husband, with History and Politics to give you something to talk about over breakfast." We both burst out laughing. She smiled grimly.

"These are talents in which I can assure you both need encouragement; as do the ability to cook, survive in extreme circumstances, defend oneself against predators, either physical or white-collar, manage your finances, understand the stock-market and money-flow, and have a reasonable knowledge of the workings of your own bodies." She paused for breath and probably to let this sink in. It did. It made complete sense to both of us.

"You would be astounded" she continued, "at the gullibility of the general public in matters concerning the acquisition of goods advertised on television, for instance, and the ease with which snake-oil nostrums are foisted on the innocent by unscrupulous firms which rely on the ignorance of the average person concerning their physical well-being. Such schemes are unfortunately only too common and the means of entrapment are extremely devious and clever. However, the prepared person who is confident of their own ability will not be under threat from such people." (I suspected that she had also been one of the unfortunate victims).

"The physical aspect of your personal security is also of paramount importance." We both nodded our agreement with this statement.

"Good," said the Assistant Headmistress, "Well, that aspect will also be taken care of and even if you never have to use any of the techniques you are taught, it will help you gain self-esteem and respect for yourself and others. Now you know more or less what our curriculum is." She paused again, apparently lost in thought. Suddenly she said,

"And we don't do religious education. How are you with horses?"

Alice said she was good with them, especially since she had been to an encounter group to deal with some childish fear. I said I was fine with them and that we were both used to riding and had mucked out for local stables during school holidays.

"Well now," she paused. "I have no wish to pry into your private lives nor have I any criticism of your relationship. I would only ask that you are extremely discreet as there are younger girls here who are not as mature as you two obviously are and it might cause them upset if they were to be subjected to anything beyond their natural understanding - if you know what I mean." I think she was slightly embarrassed at having to bring the subject up at all, and I imagine that she had been asked, possibly by the Head, to mention it, although somewhat against her will. We both assured her that our only thoughts while with the school was to absorb as much as possible the array of learning to be attained - or words to that effect - and the interview ended on this somewhat embarrassing note,

"Does she really think we're going to go around arm-in-arm snogging all over the place and wrestling each other to the ground when the passion takes us?" Alice said this in a sort of bemused voice as if she could not really believe that anybody could say such a thing. "I think it was just a mistake really," I said. I then saw that Charlie had pulled up alongside of us and heard my last remark. "Hey," she said. "Has the old Broad been giving you the sex-chat? Don't worry; we've all had it. She's ever so nice, really, but she's worried stiff that the school will get a reputation for 'Goings-On'. Well, you know what the press is like. They've got minds like sewers. Look at the way they hound people sometimes for no reason at all. Any sniff of hanky-panky and they're all coming in their pants. I can't blame her for advising us all to be Butter-Wouldn't-Melt especially when in the public eye. Maybe getting into the habit is part of the training as a lot goes on under the surface here which I'm sure you'll discover before you're much older." She glanced at her watch.

"Sorry, got to run. Things to do. Bye-ee!"

We watched her charge off and disappear into one of the classrooms. "Things to do on a Sunday? Well, well!"

"I think she improves a bit on further acquaintance," said Alice.

"I agree. Proper little mine of info, what!"

✻ ✻ ✻

One freezing October morning towards the middle of that term and after a very early breakfast, we got into our warmest winter clothes, wooly hats and all, and set out for the stables. This was the first opportunity we had had of finding some time for our riding tuition as there had been so much to assimilate in the other routines of the school. As new pupils we were obliged to have our proficiency, or lack of it, assessed by the two instructors who ran the stable yard. A couple of sturdy ponies stood patiently waiting to be saddled up and take us for what was scheduled as a gentle trot round its circumference. After that, depending on our merit, further instruction would be forthcoming. The two young men waiting with the ponies were in their very early twenties as far as I could tell. They greeted us politely and handed us each the tackle for the animals.

So far, apart from the exchange of courtesies, nobody had said anything. We saddled up and mounted the beasts. The young men made an elaborate bow indicating that the freedom of the yard was ours for the taking. We trotted round obediently, the ponies behaved with decorum and we de-ponied - elegantly and with panache. We unsaddled the beasts and gave them each a token rubdown to show willing. We then stood, waiting. Nobody spoke. We just stood and looked at each other. The ponies steamed, snorted and moseyed off to their stalls. We steamed and waited. After an interminable pause, our breaths condensing in the air in front of us, the two young men nodded their heads in unison. The darker-haired one then wrote something in his notebook. He spoke,

"'Which of you is Rachel?" he asked. I waved a finger at him.

"So you are Alice, right?" Alice nodded.

He beckoned. We followed. He took us round the stables and introduced us to the horses, all of whom were in excellent health and quite friendly and amenable.

"Pick one each and saddle up. We'll take the string out for an airing. Just walk them, OK?"

We nodded.

Half an hour later we were back in the stables and the darker-haired spoke.

"M'name's Jim and this here is Harry." We said hello politely.

"Next time we'll see how we do with a trot and maybe a canter. When's your next appointment?"

"Next Saturday, I think," replied Alice. "How long does this part go on for?"

"Until we're O.K. with the horses and we can grade you properly. Then you'll be with other rides of the same proficiency, see?"

We were silent on the way back to the main house until we were almost at the main door. Then Alice stopped.

"What do you think was going on there?" she asked. "I had the feeling that there was a sub-text somewhere that I missed."

"Of course there was,"' I replied. "You are not an innocent, young Ali. They were definitely sizing us up and trying to decide whether or not we would be favourably open to suggestions of a rather intimate nature."

"And you are rather coy, are you not, aged Rache? What you are saying is, they were wondering whether we were good for a fuck."

"Precisely, my darling Alice. The question is, are we? What did you think of them?"

"They seem like nice young men and are probably quite clean and healthy, although I don't think they've got all that much experience of women, somehow." I digested this in silence for a moment or two.

"Are you trying to say that you think there might be some of sort of relationship between them - like ours, I mean?"

"I did have that feeling, yes."

"Ooh, how interesting. But if we stay here like a couple of snowmen -"

"Ladies, please!"

"All right, snow-ladies, we'll first of all freeze to death and also people will be asking why we are standing here with silly smiles on our faces. Well, you've got a silly smile on your face," - in response to a moue from Alice, "and therefore I take it I've got a silly smile on mine. If we go in now, we might be in time for a cup of something left over from breakfast. Come along."

CHAPTER III

Alice

Our thoughts might have been much occupied by visions of the possible outcome of a more intimate occasion with the two stable lads, but the following Monday brought a new intensity to our work schedule. We had both been assessed as proficient in society manners and customs and were assured that we would be accepted as being out of the top drawer at the most rigorous entrance to high society. The relaxed few weeks had been a rather misleading calm before the storm of the new ten-hour days of intense instruction. Consequently by the time we got to our bed - we had dragged both mattresses onto the floor as a makeshift resting place - we were too exhausted to do anything but fall asleep in each other's arms. The nights seemed to be over no sooner had our heads touched the pillows and we were hard pressed to replace the mattresses, make them up, do our toilets and get dressed in time for breakfast - no longer a leisurely meal, but over by 8.25 in time for our first lessons of the day.

Fortunately the weekends were still relaxed and the leisurely breakfast and mealtimes gave us a much-needed change. None of the day students remained over the weekends, so we had a quieter and easier time without the normal hubbub of girlie chitchat.

Even though we were a bit exhausted at the end of the first week of this new regime, we decided to continue with our riding, and found ourselves part of the beginners' class which consisted of a sedate walk over the fields and surrounding areas for about an hour. The following week we had advanced to another group and from then were promoted by degrees until the boys and the advanced instructors felt confident with us. We neither of us minded this going over familiar ground too much. For one thing we were too exhausted to engage in anything beyond a canter until we had got more accustomed to both the mental and physical demands of the curriculum. Friday evenings, for instance, were set aside for martial arts instruction and we found ourselves being thrown about and physically challenged quite early on. The Fab Five, who ran these classes, were all seasoned practitioners and got quite some satisfaction in arm-locks, neck-locks and such practices; apart, that is, from the obvious joy they had on throwing us onto the floor or twisting our arms out of their sockets. We were soon also enrolled in a more advanced class that took place on Tuesday evenings. That was going to be our limit for the time being as we also had the weekly field-craft exercises.

I haven't said much about the Fab Five, mainly because the only time we first met them was on those training sessions. We found out later that they were actually five very nice Sloan Rangers who had a hilarious sense of humour and were basically extremely kind. In spite of, or perhaps because of their somewhat brutal tuition, we mastered an amount of essential techniques in a very short time and by the end of our time with them which was still a couple of years in the future, could - very occasionally - beat them at their own game, which they acknowledged with great pleasure, mostly congratulating themselves on what good teachers they were!

Just before the end-of term break, (the school ran to roughly the same schedules as normal schools), and we were getting our second wind with the school learning programme, Harry, he of the lighter hair, murmured that as next weekend there would be no official riding-class, but if we would care to drop round - it being a holiday, that is unless we had any plans and would really like to and he wasn't trying to, well, twist our arms or anything but... - so I said that I expected we would find that quite convenient - about 8.00 then? Oh sorry, too early; how about 11.00?

So there was that to look forward to!

* * *

The following Saturday we almost forgot the murmured invitation, as having the luxury of lying in bed for an extra hour - breakfast was served until 11.00 on weekends and holidays - we were making the most of our renewed energy by indulging in some gentle sensual delights. It was also a luxury to be able to watch, in daylight, our lovemaking activities in the large mirror at the end of our room. We had elected to stay over the weekend at the end of that term as neither of our parents were able to collect us until the following Monday at about mid-day.

"We've got until 11.00," breathed Rachel in my ear and, glancing at our bedside clock I saw that it was only half-past-nine.

"Oh, goodie!" I breathed back at her, "I think we should make the most of it. Shall we skip brekkers? Or crawl back later, do you think?"

"Eleven o'clock, I will be hungry by then and so will you, and --" she sat up and pulled her nightgown off, "Hey! we have a meeting with the boys, remember?"

I sprang out of bed myself. "Oh Lord, I said, "I am sooooo wet!" I grabbed myself a face flannel and scrubbed while Rachel hopped out of bed and attended to herself.

"I do so hate *coitus interruptus* don't you?" she complained.

"Well, it's a non-thing really isn't it, so not much use grumbling about it. Perhaps we could just call it To Be Continued in our Next."

"Not the same thing as you damn well know." said Rachel crossly.

I gave her a hug. "Never mind, my darling, maybe we should save something for later, don't you think? Not so good to arrive at our tryst absolutely shagged out, is it!"

She brightened up. "You do have a point."

"Well, no except for a very little one, but I expect the boys will have got quite big ones."

We went down to breakfast.

* * *

My earlier excitement and sense of euphoria diminished somewhat over breakfast. I found I was, in fact, beginning to feel intensely nervous.

"Look, Rachel," I began, "I'm not feeling all that good about this." I tried to catch her eye, but she was sort of staring into the middle-distance and seemed a bit disconnected, not only with me but also her surroundings. She grunted what sounded like an agreement.

"In fact," I continued, "I'm feeling really rather frightened. I know what Mum said to us both before we came here and that there's no chance of us becoming —" I sort of ground to a halt.

"Pregnant" said Rachel succinctly.

"Indeed."

"Well, we don't have to make a production out of it you know. Let's just play it by ear, go with the flow and if we get out of our depths we just put an end to it. They'll be as nervous as hell themselves you know."

* * *

It came back to me then very clearly what my mother had said to us as we lay in bed that Sunday morning which seemed like months ago, but was in reality only a few weeks. Rachel had been staying over as she often did at weekends - we sometimes had regular occasions when we would alternate staying at each others house - she, my mother that is, burst into the room with a cup of tea for both of us - no knocking or anything - I don't think there was any intention to catch us *in flagrante*, it was just her bull-headed way of doing everything. China shops held no terrors for her, although the reverse could not be said to hold true. I've known her send a whole display of Brummagem crockery crashing to the floor in our local emporium and causing quite a turmoil. Some parents can be so embarrassing. However, my Mum was not to be wrong-footed. Hardly had the floor manager started berating her than she drew herself to her full height of five foot one and announced in ringing tones that she was getting in touch with her lawyers immediately and suing the store for leaving hazardous displays which could cause injury and hurt to customers - bona fide customers, what's more! - and swept out with me tagging along feeling mightily put out.

Anyway, Mother came into the bedroom with the two cups of tea - (one could hear her coming a mile away, so there never was any danger of an embarrassing moment,) - and proceeded thus;

"Well you two, I know that you probably are not going to contemplate much in the way of any sort of relationship with the opposite sex at the moment, busy as you are with each other; but when you do get interested enough to find out what goes on in a boy's pants, I think you should both be prepared for the natural outcome of such an eventuality. You are both handsome and beautiful young ladies and I am sure your curiosity is just dying to be satisfied with a practical experience if you can only find yourselves a couple of nice young men to explore some exciting new sensations. Oh, I know you've explored a host of exciting and satisfying sensations already with each other - of which I thoroughly approve - but the male lover, if he proves acceptable - will provide you with a different and quite unique type of experience - that is, if he is any use as a lover! I therefore strongly advise you to go to your respective doctor's surgery and take their advice and whatever prophylaxis they deem the best to circumvent the unfortunate outcome from the results of your experiment - or, indeed, experiments. In fact I have already arranged appointments for you both with Doctors Alice Macready & Naomi Jackson."

My dearly beloved mother did not use this convoluted speechifying - she favoured a rather more direct approach. This is, in actual fact what she said,

"Look, you two, you'll soon be wanting a proper fuck before the year is out, so get yourselves on the pill now before you go." (This was a couple of weeks before we left for the school). "I've booked you in to the clinic for 8.50 and 9.00 appointments, so get your skates on."

We did, and so we were quite prepared - physically but not, unhappily, psychologically or emotionally - for what happened later. However, it was with a much lighter heart that I went to the tryst. Rachel still seemed a bit closed up. She would have these detached moments which could last anything from a few minutes to a week. I had learned early on to just sit it out and be patient - a difficult thing to be when one is young, but I managed at least a good facsimile if not always the genuine article.

* * *

The boys seemed a little shy, but the day was fine and much warmer than it had been for some weeks. The sun was shining and I thought we might just be in for a very pleasant day. And so it turned out. They had saddled our horses for us and also - surprise, surprise - fixed us all a rather nice and simple picnic with sandwiches - cheese and marmite, my favourite - and tomatoes and some fruit and flasks of coffee. What could be better?

First we went for a little canter and then, as if they had just thought of it, Harry, the fair-haired one, said oh so casually that it was almost painful, that we might care to visit their little home-from-home in the woods. Home-from-home? In the woods? Lordy, what will they think of next!

We agreed, although I must say the butterflies were beginning to kick up quite a storm and Rachel got that faraway look which denoted a certain amount of reality separation going on there. We went down a bridle path some way into Copley's Wood, or rather what was left of it after the developers had flattened it into little hovels for the proletariat; turned off into a side path and rode about half-a-mile deeper into the woods until we came to a clearing with a large barn slap-bang in the centre. The boys dismounted, helped us down and tethered the horses by a water-trough beside the front of the barn.

"C'mon," Jim said, taciturn as usual, and led the way through the doorway. Inside the place seemed enormous. It was still evidently in use as it was comparatively tidy and had that lived-in look about it - a few bales of fresh straw, some farm equipment hanging on hooks and looking as if it was kept in good condition. It smelt nice and friendly as well.

"This is our property," Harry said proudly. "We bought it from the farmer who used to own these woods. Agri-businesses bought him up, much against his will. He sold out for a good price though, and he's running an organic farm not far from here. He let us have this place for a song as long as we swore to only eat organic and to look after this old barn. Well, that was a doddle really, because that's what you get here. Proper food, not all that manufactured crap they put in supermarkets. Come on up and we'll eat upstairs and you can see our home-from-home."

"I thought you had rooms in the village," said Rachel.

"We have, but they're in different houses and we like a bit of privacy sometimes, you see," Harry explained - somewhat redundantly, I thought. By this time we had climbed the ladder to the platform which ran across the length of the stalls below. It was a comfortable roomy space. Under the eaves lay a large double mattress which was nicely furnished with bed linen, blankets and a magnificent patchwork quilt.

"Made that, us did," commented Jim and led the way to a small dining table with four chairs and some plates and cutlery attendant. We sat ourselves down and Jim poured us out some coffee.

"You OK with coffee?" asked Harry. "We haven't got everything running yet, but should have some water up here soon when we can get time to plumb it in. We do with rain-water mostly and a camping-stove if we're going to be here for any length of time."

"Come summer break we'll be here most times," Jim said, making that the longest contribution to any conversation we had so far had with him. After we had finished our meal and chatted a bit and tidied up a bit, we gravitated almost seamlessly to the large and inviting mattress which I think had been beckoning us all unconsciously since we arrived. It was certainly the centre of attention with the wonderfully coloured quilt quite overshadowing any of the other pieces of furniture in the loft.

I found myself paired off with Harry and Rachel seemed happy with the taciturn Jim. I think we were all a little nervous and shy of each other and were oddly enough seemingly content with just a bit of gentle snogging. I could hear Jim's voice rumbling away into Rachel's ear. He obviously found her a sympathetic listener. Harry was burbling away about his schooldays and I was lulled into a contented dozy state in between bouts of kissing and gentle mutual fondling with my nice-smelling partner. I could feel his erection when we sort of rolled together, but he would pull himself away from me when our bodies touched. I imagine he was on the verge of ejaculation and was feeling somewhat worried about it. I, on the other hand, would have loved to have seen him coming but I sympathised with the thought that if he came in his trousers the telltale stains might prove very embarrassing. I wondered whether I should in fact say anything about the situation, as for example; "That's OK, just take your trousers off and come all over me!" or perhaps, "Would you like me to give you a blow-job?" But I didn't. I behaved like a nice well brought up English girl and pretended not to notice his tumescence, even though I was dying to know what it would be like to have his cock in my mouth and experience his climax. Rachel and I had watched one or two blue movies, so we did have a good idea of what happened between heterosexual couples - or threesomes - or foursomes, whatever! Because, of course, that was going to happen one day. We would all be playing daisy chains and multiple orgasms and group sex and I would have one cock up me, and another in my mouth and totally beside myself with climactic lust! Boy oh boy!

And with that thought I drifted off into a lovely warm place. Harry was cuddling me and kissing me gently and I was swooning about having lascivious and libidinous imaginings abut these poor innocent boys who probably wanted just to get back to each other really, so wasn't it time we went home?

The next thing I knew was that I was on my own in the bed - somebody had covered me with the quilt - and the other three were finishing off the last of the coffee and chattering away together nineteen to the dozen. I lay where I was for some minutes longer, just enjoying the warmth and the companionable sounds of the others. I think they were making arrangements for the following term and perhaps going a bit further afield before coming back here. I got out of the bed and went over to the table and sat next to Rachel. I wasn't quite awake yet and was content to let her make all the arrangements. We decided to call it a day then and return to the school. By now it was getting on for suppertime and I was suddenly very hungry. All that imagination and cerebral activity and just a couple of cheese and marmite sandwiches and coffee. Not really enough for a growing girl.

CHAPTER IV

Rachel

We got back to the school in good time for supper. Alice was almost foaming at the mouth with hunger, or perhaps it was with something else as the analogy is not really applicable to starvation. One doesn't, I imagine, foam at the mouth if one is hungry so maybe she was just foaming at the mouth with frustrated sexual desire. I was meditating this as we sat down to eat.

"You, actually," I remarked quietly to Alice, "are, in fact, a nymphomaniac."

"Oho!" she responded pertly, "And what does my Lady and Mistress of my heart mean by that quindisyllabic utterance?"

"Touchy! Also, I don't think there's any such word."

"I've just responded to a lacuna in the Lexicon by coining a particular taxonomic label," she responded smugly. "Also, touchy with reason. Are you including yourself in this category?"

"Could be," I admitted. "I was certainly engaged in thoughts which are only appropriate for communicating to my closest and dearest friend and of a nature unbecoming to the mind of a young person of good breeding. I don't think I could even utter them towards the objects of my very own personal lust - so far, anyway. Perhaps when we get to know them better there could be an appropriate moment to voice some confidences."

"Coo, posh talk!" Our large freckled friend Charlie had just joined us. She was staying on during the holiday period for some reasons that were not very clear, probably because she didn't mean them to be. My opinion of her was growing. Beneath all the schoolgirl facade lurked, I suspected, a very sharp brain which had created an ideal silly juggins persona to hide behind. If I was right about this then either she was older than we realised or she was very mature for her age.

"Actually the word is quinquesyllabic, just so as you know," Charlie remarked casually not looking either of us in the eye. There was a pregnant silence.

"I see," aid Alice. "So you heard our little conversation."

"Well, I really couldn't help it, you know. I've got extremely sharp hearing." Charlie was very contrite. "Anyway, I promise not to mention it to anybody. But if," she continued a little hesitantly, "If you ever need any advice, you can always ask the Fab Five. They're ever so discreet and helpful. I know because I had a problem last term and they cleared it up in no time for me."

"Well, thanks, Charlie" I said. "That's very good to know. We seem to be getting on with them at training class very well and we do like them a lot."

"Oh, super," Charlie was back in jolly hockey-sticks mode now.

"So, what's your day been like?" Alice asked. The conversation then took a turn for the worse and consisted of a blow-by-blow account of a girls' football match in which Charlie had featured as goal-keeper. No doubt to those interested in football it would have only been somewhat tedious; to me and, I think from the look on her expressionless face, to Alice, it was pure Purgatory. What one does to keep one's friends happy and discreet!

* * *

"Never, never, never let us allow the word football to pass her lips again," Alice was fulminating as we arranged our mattresses later. "I know, it was for the good of the cause, discretion and all that, and she's a sweetheart, but I swear to God that if she starts on a breakdown of every goal she saved and what the team did and how many fouls there were, I shall sit on her head - preferably when I'm having my period. I'll be more in the mood then!"

"Hush, darling, it's all over now and we can have a lovely little time together and forget about Charlie. I think she's really rather clever and also reliable, so let's just pretend we're being screwed senseless by those two beautiful boys. I wonder," I mused, "what they are doing now."

"Oh, probably whizzing away at either themselves or each other, I expect. That's if they didn't do it just after we left them. And you," she added, "were also salivating over them, weren't you?"

"Indeed and I also think a little micturition was in process as well."

"How scientific and clever of you, my love. Let's us have some beautiful sex together as I'm feeling as randy as an old goat."

"Well, as long as you don't start smelling like one that's fine by me."

"I think it's my turn to have my hair brushed isn't it?" Alice pleaded. "Or shall we skip that tonight?"

"No, let's do it. I'm fairly knackered but you had a kip this afternoon you naughty creature!"

She sighed, "Yes, we must have foreplay. Would it were four play! That's a literary joke," she added.

"Please. You are as bad as Charlie. Come sit on the chair then."

I brushed her golden tresses and I'm not going into any more details except to say that next morning, which was a Sunday, we did not wake until well after breakfast was over and done with. Later that morning, the weather being warm enough for a spring day, we went for a leisurely walk on the moors. Dartmoor is one of the most beautiful places on earth - when the sun is shining! It can also turn into one of the most alarming and even terrifying when enveloped in fog or cloud and one loses the path. The risk of falling into a bog is also very high on the list of things not to do in Dartmoor. Consequently we were back at the school gates well in time for tea. It grows dark round about 4.00 at that time of the year and having lived most of our lives in the area we were well aware of the vagaries of the local climate.

Next day, bang on time, my parents, Rebecca and Joseph arrived to take us home for Christmas.

* * *

As neither of our families is at all religious, we spent Christmas, as do most agnostics and atheists, in a riot of worship of the Great God Mammon. It didn't snow that year. In fact the mild and sunny weather we had experienced on our last full day at the school continued well over the holiday period. Three days into the New Year and my parents drove us back to the walled village. The weather had finally broken and it looked as if we were in for some serious wet. In fact by the time we arrived it was coming down in buckets - straight down with no let-up just like a monsoon in fact. Joseph commented on it. "Climate change, I reckon, don't you?" he addressed the world at large. As there were only the four of us in the car we treated the question as rhetorical. My mother ventured some observation about how it rains like this continually in Manchester, her home town, but both Alice and I were too full of Christmas leftovers, including puddings and cakes, that we had no energy left for conversation. We staggered out of the car, kissed my loving parents goodbye, and staggered up to our rooms.

""I think I need a vomitorium and then a colonic irrigation," I grumbled.

"So, you need an exit from the Colosseum, do you?" my friend enquired. "And it's more polite to say colonic hydrotherapy. Irrigation is what you do for field crops."

"Don't be a smart Alec, or should it be smart Alice?"

I lay down beside her and we were both asleep before Jack Robinson's name could have been uttered.

* * *

Our first class on the Monday of the new term was with our lovely headmistress. She had a knack of focusing her class's mind so well on the subject in hand, that residual thoughts of our previous activities were immediately banished in favour of the day's subject. Today was Comparative History & Politics, one of the few subjects we studied together, which was also mandatory along with Health, Nutrition and one or two other kindred disciplines. And so the week continued and I think we both did as well as we could to keep up with the course, which was very fast in spite of the layer of calm and control which governed the running of the school. They were all first class teachers and we found we were being constantly inspired and encouraged to develop our natural abilities. It was a truly wonderful institution and the near tragedy that would have ended it all should never have happened. However, there's always a downside to stuff happening as well as an upside and we were learning to focus on the upside.

Louise was, in our opinion, the most approachable - for confidences, that is - of the Five. We managed to detach her from the others after the following Friday's Hurling Us About The Gymnasium session was over. (Gymnasium was originally a place where one exercised naked - those old Greeks, what!)

Louise heard out our little petition concerning how to proceed with shy young men lusted after by shy young ladies, and in her opinion we were doing just fine. Take your time, was her advice, and never pressurise or get worried about the situation. Remember that us girls had got something the boys haven't got very much of, and that - here she fixed a beady eye on Alice who was exhibiting signs of anticipation - is patience. We should at all times be relaxed and compliant with the chaps. Any forward behaviour, such as fumbling around in their trousers, talking dirty - we raised our eyebrows at that! - or taking your clothes off before they were ready for it might result in the sort of bad attitude and behaviour that we young ladies so dislike in our menfolk. (She really did use those words, in a sort of mock severe, mother superior way.}.

After the preliminaries were over, she continued, and the serious foreplay had started we would just have to use our instincts as to when to completely open up to our passion. Remember, she added, that these two are presumably in a relationship and probably a bit sensitive themselves about the outcome of this new alliance with yourselves and could quite easily be scared off back into each others arms and yourselves back to square one. So don't be possessive. It's probably a good idea to swap partners and even have a little flirtation with each other from time to time to reassure them that their feelings for each other are in no way threatened. I take it that you are also in a friendly sort of way with them, chatting away happily about this and that? We nodded. Good, because that is also essential for good intimate relationships. If they are based solely on sexual activity then there is nothing to fall back on when you want to stop and have a cup of tea, is there? This will also safeguard any disturbance to yourselves and your relationship because there's always a danger in these situations that distrust or jealousy will take hold of any one of you and that would be a great misfortune.

And with that she suddenly attacked the two of us with the unsurprising result that we were not only very surprised but also flat on our backs and completely winded. Be Prepared!

"Never mind, you'll learn," were her final words of the evening as she helped us up.

* * *

After a late supper we were in our room sitting on the bed and manicuring - or should it be pedicuring - each other's toes. We had got into this habit since our picnic day with the boys, sort of prettying ourselves up a bit - not make-up or anything ghastly like that - but generally tidying ourselves up and dressing a bit better. Hoydenish behaviour was fine for us on our own, but I think men like to have girlie-looking girls around - makes them feel manly and superior, or protective or whatever.

"I don't know whether I really enjoy this very much," Alice grumbled. "Why are we doing this exactly? Do you think they would like us any the less if we were just ourselves?"

"Well, this is just ourselves, isn't it? Doing girlie things together?"

"Bollocks!"

"Oh, very well, do your own toes then. I thought this might have been easier."

"OK, I'm just feeling a bit out of sorts. That last throw was really out of order.."

"Yeah, they take being prepared really seriously, don't they? For our own good, you know." Alice grunted. "Don't you remember when Harry came and gave us some training? Just before we had that confrontation with those boys at school? We were as sharp as knives then. Have we lost our edge, do you think?"

"Yes I do, and this is a wake-up call, Alice, so bite the bullet. We've lost the edge because we don't expect our friends to attack us. Also we're not keeping up our own practice enough. The truth is we're getting a bit too much used to being in a gang and not relying entirely on ourselves. It's all very well being part of a team as long as we're 100% as sure of them as we are of each other. We've been getting a bit sleepy and also lulled into a false sense of security."

"We certainly don't seem to be at the top of our game these days. The thing is we need to trust them and they are on our side, so what does one do?"

"Just keep awake, is all. If we had been totally awake we wouldn't have both been caught out. It's because we were thinking about our own selfish little problems and had lost the plot rather and Louise did us a kindness. If we hadn't been wrapped up in our hormones at least one of us would have downed her, if not both of us."

"Well, I think it's a bit much when one of your best friends suddenly ups at you with a meat cleaver, I don't think! Who needs friends like that anyway!"

"Alice, that is not the point. It's being always and ever vigilant and aware and even prescient about any eventuality. It's for our own good you know. You remember what that WuShu instructor told us at the first class?"

"Yes, I know and I'm sorry. I'm just feeling in a rotten mood tonight and being thrown about by Louise right in the middle of a friendly discussion - it seems, I don't know - a bit like treachery really."

It was obvious that Alice was very upset and I thought that any minute now she was going to burst into tears. It happened from time to time that some pressure built up in her that needed release and she hadn't found a way of dealing with it yet, except by losing her cool and becoming miserable. I knew better than to try and comfort her in this state. She could not bear to be touched; the only solution I had found to date was to put the kettle on, make her a hot drink and leave her alone. Unfortunately we didn't have a kettle. I did have an idea though.

"Come down to the gym with me?" I suggested. "What the fuck for?" she demanded. "Do you want to practice your Let's Chuck Alice on the Floor routine?"

"Not exactly. Would you come?" Alice, still surly, got up and we went down to the gym. Everybody else had gone by then, of course. The Five used to go down to the Black Swan of a Friday evening after class, which was a mile or so away and really needed a car, which of course they had. Strictly speaking they each had a vehicle but they would usually pile into Beattie's Beamer 5 series and stay until closing time. They didn't drink much, usually only a shandy or small glass of wine, which they would make last the whole evening. We had been invited with the rest of the class during the inauguration evening at the beginning of that term, but never since and none of us wanted or expected it, principally as we were so knackered at the end of a session with the girls that it was cocoa time and straight to bed.

This evening was a bit different. Alice was in a mood and I felt restless myself.

We turned on the lights and I opened one of the cupboards where the sporting equipment was kept and got out a pair of boxing gloves for Alice. She tried them on and they fitted well enough.

"Okay," I said, "Let's just do a warm-up with the punch bag." I got behind it as I had seen so many people do on the movies, and told Alice to start punching. Alice is no stranger to boxing. She did it in the last year at our secondary school and fared pretty well even against some of the more experienced opponents.

"Fire away," I said blithely. And Alice fired away. After that I put on gloves myself and we did some practice sparring and then a couple of rounds of a fairly friendly match. She had by then managed to work off most of her anger and unhappiness, and now we both needed hot showers, rub down and a bit of massage.

"I think we'll have to get a kettle and some tea things in here," Alice remarked later as I was massaging her back and shoulders. "Do you think anybody would mind?"

"I don't think there's any need to tell them," I replied. "If we keep all the doings at the back of our wardrobe in boxes nobody need ever know. And if they do find out by any chance," I added, "We can just plead simple-minded ignorance. I don't think there are any rules about it. In fact, I think we could probably keep a couple of AK47s in here as far as the rule-book goes."

"Wouldn't look good on our term reports and CVs would it, though." Alice rolled over on her back. "Do my feet and legs please," she said. "I mean, fancy having a school report which read; History and Mathematics A plus, but subject was arrested by Special Branch before the end of the spring semester for having a concealed weapon in her bedroom and is now serving a life sentence! I don't think Daddy - or even Mummy - would be too pleased. And poor Miss Davison would be terribly shocked."

"AK47s? Not at all nice! I think something more needs doing concerning your present angst, don't you?"

Alice mumbled something about being a bit tired but relaxed now thank you very much.

"Just get under the blankets and shut your eyes. I'll be with you in a moment."

"Okay", she murmured happily, "I can wait."

Last year we had had gone on a little shopping spree up to London and visited the Ann Summers shop in Soho and treated ourselves to some choice toys which had taken our fancy. I was busy strapping one onto myself. We don't use them very often mainly because we're not really very fond of Latex and also there's no need. In this case, however, I decided it might be just what the doctor ordered - my Strapadictomy - not original, I know, but the old ones are the best - or so they say.

Alice looked happily tucked up for the night, but I was by now fairly aroused. I folded the bedclothes back, which revealed Alice's right hand playing with her clitoris and her left hand caressing her right nipple. I gently spread her legs further apart and brought my lips down on the place where her right hand was playing. She put her fingers in my mouth and I tasted the sex on them. This aroused me even more and moving my mouth up her body sought her lips and we kissed deeply. She then transferred her hands to my breasts and started to tweak my nipples, knowing full well the effect it would have on me. I guided the dildo into her vagina and gently pushed it in as far as it would go. She gave a great gasp and almost shouted, "Oh, it's so big!" and clutched me so tightly in her embrace that I felt we were one person.

"Hush," I murmured in her ear. "You'll frighten the horses, let alone wake the neighbours."

Alice giggled and held me even tighter. Our thrusting movements became more energetic and before long we were thrashing about almost uncontrollably. They really are good, these double- headed dildos and I had a fleeting thought that I should let Ann Summers know what a lot of pleasure we were having. However any passing fancies were soon submerged in the totality of the event and we were both climaxing, relaxing then climaxing again - and again, until we eventually fell into a deep and happy sleep entwined in each others loving arms.

* * *

I believe there is supposed to be some difference in the male experience of sexual activity from that experienced by the female of the species. Apparently us girls get completely lost in it if all goes well, but men can still keep a detached part of themselves observing the proceedings with a cool and wintry eye. Makes you think, don't it! I also think I will ask the boys about this - when, that is, we have got to know each other a bit better.

CHAPTER V

Alice

O ur hopes of following up on the events of our last meeting with our stable friends was dashed owing to an invitation we couldn't refuse. The following Saturday our belovèd headmistress, the exquisitely groomed and charming Lucy Davison (Miss and not Ms!), had placed - I could not imagine her doing this in person - on each of our tidily made beds, (which had probably not fooled her or her messenger for one moment), a discreetly gilded card inviting us to a tea-party at which the honoured guest was none other than our patron, the prince of that far-Eastern caliphate and of which I have mentioned at the opening of these chronicles. R.S.V.P. *naturellement!* - and dress suitable for the occasion. An honoured guest was also the prince's cousin, Bahir, who had been the architect responsible for the refurbishment of the school some years previously.

Here I should perhaps say a word about our general attitude towards sartorial elegance, or in our case, lack of it. Our usual get-up was gym-shoes, sweatshirts with tracksuit bottoms covered by any lairs of jumpers or cardigans deemed necessary to keep out the cold. Well, it was a comfortable and practical outfit for general use. Seeing how much we were chucked about each week by martial arts, field-games, gymnastics, horse-riding and other activities, it was the generally accepted wear for most of the advanced students. We also had survival training, a number of these sessions being held in the surrounding countryside. None of these activities were mentioned in the syllabus. They were mostly subsumed under the heading of P.E. (physical education), sports, cadet training (optional).

We gave quite some thought to what to wear for the tea-party and eventually decided on one of Laura Ashley's most becoming cotton frocks for Rachel and a beautiful silk dress for me, which totally turned me on just by thinking about it. We both had a small but exciting selection of lingerie and, truth be told, this was the first occasion we had had to wear anything so sensually satisfying and seductive. Denim and linen and cotton are OK for working wear but, when one wants to revel in one's femininity and wow the audience, there's nothing like some good old-fashioned dresses - coming well below the knee, even ankle-length - and fashioned in soft and warm-coloured silks. We bathed and trimmed each other's hair and spent the whole of that Saturday morning preparing ourselves for the afternoon. Naturally there was never any application of cosmetics of any sort. (How some women can smother themselves with expensive unguents, creams, mascara, rouge and all the other paraphernalia is beyond me. It all smells so awful as well and the taste must surely put off any potential suitors - of either sex!). We used coconut oil as moisturiser and hair tonic, rubbed ourselves down with a towel and stepped into our silken underwear, stockings and outer garments and were all ready, like Cinders, for the ball with half-an-hour to spare.

(A good tip for a bit of foreplay is to have a nice warm bath or shower together, dry yourselves off and then, placing the towels on the bed, floor or wherever you want to be, have a bottle of olive oil to hand. Coconut oil is also good if you don't want to get too greased up, but olive is best and also very nutritious for the skin. Then smother each other with the oil, not neglecting the most sensitive and responsive parts of the body and massage in well. The longer you take with each other, the more satisfying the whole process is. Just be careful you don't get any of the oil in your eyes as it is not a very pleasant experience and would seriously spoil your mutual enjoyment!)

Rachel shone like a warm summer's day in her printed Laura Ashley - how I loved that woman's designs! And I? I looked like a magic being who had just woken up to her sexuality. Well, that's what I thought of myself when we stood side by side in front of the long mirror at the end of our room, hand in hand like I don't know what - certainly not Babes in any Wood! I was feeling so turned on by the feel of all this silk close my skin that I was almost wetting myself. Seeing Rachel so gorgeously enclosed in the warm reds of her dress and also recent memories of her climbing into her lingerie did nothing to cool my ardour. However. I managed to pull myself together and turned to her. I kissed her chastely on the lips and my heart spoke the words for me. "I love you so much"

Rachel kissed me back gently and said, very quietly, "And I love and adore you."

Feeling absolutely on top of the world we floated out of the room, down the stairs and along the corridor to the large hall.

* * *

If one wants to make an entrance which freezes all the activity in a given space, one has to make sure that everybody else has already arrived and that there is no possibility of a late arrival upstaging you at the critical moment. This is naturally either a matter of luck, good management or such awesome charisma as to negate anybody else having any effect whatsoever. With us it was obviously good luck. We entered quietly side by side, not touching each other, stood surveying the assembled company and waited. Silently and without movement or ostentation. Merely surveying the crowd with gentle patience. We were rewarded.

Slowly all the chatter died down, the tea-cups stopped rattling, the ones already on their way to already parted lips were frozen in mid-flight; cups already raised steamed gently on to the misty glasses of those in mid-sip; those on the downward path from lately refreshed mouths were halted in mid-air as if their imbibers had turned to stone. Others, unladen by china bearing liquid, holding cake, sandwich or biscuit, were equally petrified. It was as if, during one of those dynamic meditations so loved of by the Bhagwan Shree Rajneesh, a voice had intoned the booming command "STOP!" which caused the chelas and other participants to instantly remain in the positions they found themselves - even if it were in mid-flight. The thumping, hypnotic music would suddenly stop; there would be a dead silence and at that point the more fortunate seekers after enlightenment would find their souls flying from their corporal bodies and merging with the One! The less fortunate would overbalance and fall painfully and noisily floorwards!

Happily for the guests on this occasion nobody dropped so much as a teaspoon and after what was probably only a few seconds (it only seemed like an eternity) the headmistress detached herself from a small group of people and came forward to welcome us.

"Come along, my dears," she said, completely unfazed as usual. "You both look absolutely beautiful and I am most gratified that you have taken so much trouble over your appearance. It always helps to make a good impression on our noble patron," she murmured quietly as she walked between us and held our elbows to gently steer us towards the prince.

"Your Highness, may I present Rachel Katz and Alice Darwin whom I know you have already met. Rachel is studying General Science and Alice has chosen Literature and Languages. They have, I think, settled down very well in the short time that they have been here."

She smiled benevolently at us, although I thought I detected a little something of a secret behind the smile. Nothing negative, more of a sort of amiable complicity. I could have been mistaken.

"Oh come, Lucy. Let's not be formal," the Prince was all charm and warmth. "I have many given names, but my favourite is Salim. It means one who is peaceful and happy."

"That is very kind of you, Salim," our principal replied. "Rachel, Alice, I shall leave you with His Highness - Salim, - so that you may tell him about some of your activities since your arrival. With your permission, Salim."

Had she put the subtlest of stresses on "some of your activities"? I wondered, or was that just paranoia? I would have to discuss this with Rachel later. Meanwhile, on with the plot. Salim was quizzing Rachel about which aspect of the General Sciences was of particular interest to her. I stood observing him while he was chatting and came to the conclusion, *pro tem*, that he was what he appeared to be: charming, warm-hearted and interested in us as members of his school and genuinely benign. He then turned to me and talked Literature and Classics and slowly but skillfully drew us into a cosy little threesome so that it was not long before we found that we were just like old friends chatting away together and completely at ease with ourselves. Pure magic.

Later when we discussed the day we agreed that it had been one of the nicest and most interesting parties we had ever been to. Salim knew how to make friends and influence people. We both felt that we would do almost anything for him; probably because he had so convinced us of his genuineness that he would never ask anything that was beyond our abilities, our conscience or our wishes. The same could not be said of the impression we had of his cousin Bahir. His name might mean bright or dazzling, but neither of us was illuminated nor dazzled by him. We both felt that Bahir, the architect, somehow had a very dark wolf inside of him, which he fed more than any of the other wolves he might have lurking there.

That evening ended very pleasantly for both of us, though some of the lingerie got a bit torn in places. Looking back on it of course, I realise that this was the seed from which an appalling and horrendous flower was to grow.

* * *

The next day, being a Sunday and with some leisure time available, we wandered round to the stables to see if the boys were about and free for some jolly bits of intimacy, but there was no sign of them. An older man was mucking out the stables and generally doing things that older men do around horses. He didn't seem ecstatic to see us.

"Stables is closed Sundays," he grunted, barely looking at us.

"We hoped to have a word with Jim if he was around," Rachel said mildly.

"Well, he ain't, nor t'other one neither," was the response.

"OK," Rachel waggled her fingers at him and we walked on.

"Shall we try their barn?" I asked. Rachel shook her head. "I somehow think that would not be a good idea. Something tells me that all is not very copacetic in the air at the moment."

"Americanisms yet! Where did you get that one from, pray? I think you've been watching too much television recently."

"So, what is wrong with introducing an unfamiliar word into the conversation? Do we have to continue just using the familiar? Or shall we strive to be original and interesting. That way we can broaden the mind and increase our desire to understand others and go where no human woman has gone before. To delve into the miracles and iniquities that abound in countless universes, to explore the galaxies of imagination that lie within the confines of the brain, to step outside one's cave. Travel with me while I investigate the mysterious and the unknown."

"Why don't you just shut the fuck up?"

"Oh, all right, then."

She took my arm and we went for an amiable stroll through the village. We had not really had the time or energy to explore the village to date, so it was with interest that we looked about us. We had got as far as the Post Office-cum-convenience store, which lay at the heart of a cluster of thatched cottages of some antiquity that surrounded it. There didn't seem to be a soul about, but I thought it possible they were either in church, or more likely, the pub. Even, mayhap, preparing Sunday lunch for those in either place. The hanging sign outside had a recently painted picture of a horse and cart standing somnolently & motionless outside a building which closely resembled the Horse & Cart which depicted the very sign outside the building portraying the very pub we were standing outside at that particular moment in time which in turn had a minuscule hanging sign which .... I wrenched my eyes away from it.

"Hmm, very clever and very well painted. I wonder what bright artist did that." Rachel was quite enchanted with it.

I suggested we go inside and get to know some of the locals and find out. Perhaps we might be luckier with them than we were being with the boys. (I am beginning to seriously consider whether I have a problem with nymphomania. I put the proposition to Rachel.)

"No, my mind travels in the same way. It's just natural in girls - and boys - of our age group," she replied. "I wouldn't worry about it. You'll feel better after you been fucked silly by some bloke with a big schlong. Let's go in and have a drink. I think we need one."

Making the sort of entrance that freezes time itself could come to be a habit. Oddly enough this time nobody took the slightest notice of us apart from the barman. We ordered halves of bitter and looked around the bar for a familiar face. The bar itself was a one room affair. Quite large and with a log fire dominating what had probably been the saloon before open plan grabbed everybody's imagination. Nope, no familiar faces.

"Who painted your sign outside?" Rachel asked the barman. "You better ask the governor about that," he replied. "I'm only temporary here, see, as I don't live in the village, and he'll know all about it. Bloke called Carter I think. Clever innit?"

We nodded our thanks to him and went over to sit by the fire. The place wasn't too full but as it had obviously just opened a few minutes ago, the main characters were most probably the regulars whom you can see at any village pub who usually arrive before opening time and are first in when the landlord unbolts the door. However it was beginning to fill up and consequently get a bit noisier. About thirty minutes later we were just getting prepared to get our coats on and leave the pub - nobody had shown the slightest interest in us and the landlord hadn't appeared yet - when Harry and Jim walked in the door. They touched their caps to us and came over.

"Hello, you two. We've just been down to the stable to see if you were around today, but there was just this older guy who didn't seem all that pleased to see us, so —"

"Yes, we've just spoken to Bert," Harry said. He stood there fiddling with his cap. Both the boys looked a bit sheepish and embarrassed.

"Come on, out with it," I said, somewhat snappishly, I'm afraid. "You don't want to get involved with us, is that it?"

Both the boys' faces flushed with anger or resentment or some other emotion which I couldn't fathom.

"No, no. Look, it's not like that at all." Harry as usual was speaking for them both. Jim just stood there looking dolefully at the floor in front of him. "It's - well, it's - er - it's like this."

There was a dead silence - from Harry anyway. The hubbub around was getting noisier every moment.

"Look," Harry began. We waited.

More silence from the pair. At last —-

"It's like this," - we waited, expectant. ""We've been warned off you - there!"

We looked at each other. We looked back at Harry. We looked at Jim. We looked at Harry again.

"Would you care to elaborate on that a bit more fully?' asked Rachel in her deadliest of quiet voices.

Jim spoke. It was quite a revelation because all we'd heard from Jim in the short time we had know the two boys, was either mutterings in Rachel's ear - she had never divulged what the mutterings were! - and various grunts at appropriate times in confirmation of something Harry had said. Now his speech was clear, sturdy and articulate, but voiced at a level only we could hear.

"We've been warned off you by our bosses - not old Bert, who's a good sort once you get to know him. No, it comes from the top. You are not to be fraternised with. Those were the exact words, otherwise we will be chucked out and our barn razed to the ground and we'll be lucky not to be in it. That was the message, and believe you me we had no option but to take it to heart. Don't ask me why. We don't want this, but we have no option, unless we put all four of us in danger. So, we're very sorry because we both like you very much and we also fancy you rotten. Just so as you know." Jim knuckled his head at us, signaled to Harry and the two of them walked straight out of the bar.

We did our coats up slowly, put on our little wooly hats and followed them out. They had completely disappeared by the time we got outside. We walked slowly way from the pub continuing away from the school end of the village.

"I didn't notice anybody eying us up while that was going on, did you?' I ventured after some minutes. Rachel pursed her lips. "No, but - vanity aside - I think it a bit odd that absolutely not one single person gave us so much as the once-over, don't you? All those men in there, two attractive unaccompanied females enter the bar and not one of them even eyes them up in the bar mirror? Are they all screaming queens? Homosexuals treated with aversion therapy to non-react to the female of the species? Gay to the point of lunacy?"

"Something is afoot, Watson!" I said, adopting a pretty inaccurate Sherlockian pose. "Is it the game? Or is it this piece of dog-turd which I have found attached to my shoe? Think, Watson. When the improbable is exhausted, all that is left is the impossible!"

"Very interesting, but surely the Head would never issue such a diktat? It must have come from the Prince, as I assume that he has the ultimate power in the running of the school."

I mulled this over as we rambled on rather listlessly.

"The thing is, I can not imagine that charming man issuing blood-curdling threats like that to anybody, let alone a couple of stable lads and about something which is really not anybody's business but ours. And how did he, whoever he is - I assume a 'he' - find out about us. 'He' must have spies or eyes around all over the place."

"Weird," Rachel agreed. "Well, I'm sorry about the lads as they seem to be a nice couple and we might have had some good times with them, but it's not worth endangering them or their lovely barn because we are selfish hedonistic little trollops."

"Indeed not," I said. "But what we can do is to have a jolly good walk, then a jolly good lunch and then go bed together and have a jolly good fuck and do you think we should discuss the matter with our lovely headmistress?"

"Discuss our proposed fuck, you mean? I hardly think Lucy Davison is the person to discuss our sex-life with, do you? The Headmistress of our lovely school, who probably is having a lovely time with our lovely patron, both of whom we have agreed have nothing to do with this, and if we informed them might find themselves in quite a quandary. Would they feel it incumbent upon themselves, as guardians of our morals as well as of our educational development, to dismiss the two gentlemen in question and then perhaps to enquire too closely into our own relationship with the subsequent upheaval that would inevitably cause? Pray consider, Miss Darwin."

Well, I did consider and, as it turned out, the wisest course would have been to go straight to Lucy Davison, which might have saved not only ourselves but also Lucy Davison herself one terrifyingly awful experience. We did think however, that Louise, she of the Fab Five, might point us in the right direction of the source of this threat. But that was for another day. Our immediate need was for a refreshing and blood stimulating walk, a jolly good slap-up lunch, and then some trollopy times in our own little sex-haven. There's a place near Brighton called Peacehaven, which is full of little boxes housing the elderly on their final journey to the Great Box in the Sky. When I grow rich and famous and have so much money I don't know what to do with, I will found a small village somewhere in the sun in a foreign clime, and call it Sexhaven.

Brave New World!

CHAPTER VI

Rachel

The following Friday evening we were both tucked into a cosy little nook in the Groom & Dragon which was some fifteen miles outside the village on the way to Nowhere Much. I don't know how the girls, or indeed any of the other occupants, had found the place, but it was very busy with apparently well-to-do professionals. What their professions were was not very obvious though it was friendly enough and very unlike our village pub with its quite weird atmosphere. After we had brought the subject up with Louise at the end of the following Friday session, without saying anything she had beckoned us out to her car, (a rather swish-looking Saab) and asked us if we minded if Twinky came along for the ride. Twinky was a small black-haired little creature with pigtails who looked about 12 years old, but was in reality exactly double that age. We were only too pleased to have her along as she had a quite delightful sense of naughty humour which seemed to shine through all her activities.

"OK, shoot," said Louise after we had at last got served at the crowded bar. We shot.

"Wow," said Twinky when we had finished. "Pretty heavy duty. GBH and death-threat combinations - not good for the soul."

"Or the body," Louise added.

"Especially the body. Ugh! I don't think that came from either the Prince or the Head. In fact, it would be impossible for either of them to act like that. If they didn't want you to associate with those boys then they would have found a much subtler way."

"I totally agree," said Louise. "This is the workings of a thuggish mind. Who do we know with that sort of attitude? And what connection do they have with the school? Or with either of you or those boys? And what's the purpose of it all?"

We sat there silently. I picked my half pint of beer and took a sip or two. The others also decided to discuss their drinks.

"There is one person, and it's the only one I can think of, who might do this," Alice said slowly. "Have either of you met Bahir, the Prince's cousin? Architect guy who did the overhaul of the building some years ago?" Both Twinkly and Louise shook their heads. "We weren't here then. Where did you meet him?" asked Louise.

"Weren't either of you at that tea party the other day - last Saturday?" Alice asked the two older girls. "The Prince introduced us to him. Wouldn't shake hands, merely bowed stiffly at us. About five foot eight, slight build, Eastern features, not exactly handsome but certainly rather spooky; to my mind anyway. What did you think, Rachel?"

"Definitely sent warning signals up my spine. Wouldn't trust him an inch," I replied confidently. "Also he gave off the vibes of a really angry person. Not much tolerance towards women there I would say. Kitchen/bedroom sort of misogyny I reckon."

Louise said, "We were at the party all right but didn't get much of a chance to speak to the Prince, mainly because he seemed to be fascinated with you two. Quite an entrance you made. Congratulations! We thought you were just two good little girls and butter wouldn't melt and we discovered that you are potential divas of some potency."

"Hey," Alice said laughingly, "It was pure spirit of the moment. We'd spent all day prettying ourselves up, got on a high and went for it just as we got to the hall. *Carpe diem!* You know."

"Fair enough," Twinky smiled at us. "And you did look absolutely ravishing. I wanted to eat you all up - both of you. Great big gorgeous sex-bombs, you two!"

"Whoa! Steady on, girl!" Louise laid a hand on her arm. "Remember where you are. Don't startle the horses."

"That's just what we said to each other the other - OW!" Alice glared at me from across the table and rubbed her ankle.

"There's a lot of it about," Twinky remarked sadly, reverting to an earlier part of the conversation. "There must still be about a continent-size number of males who think that women are sinks, literally, of iniquity, and only good for relieving themselves into and using them like pocket handkerchiefs. Gurdjieff came out with that one half a century ago. I think that guy had humanity sussed out pretty good. I don't know where they get all this shit from, but it seems to me..........."

"Twinky, please don't get on your soapbox," Louise interrupted her. "Let's try and find out which arsehole is behind this. I suppose," she ventured turning to us, "that the boys - what are their names?"

"Harry and Jim," Alice supplied.

"Yes, Harry and Jim. Of course, the two stable-lads. Nice boys. I thought they had a thing going with each other?"

"Yes, well, we - er - " I started and then dried up.

"Of course, this was the 'problem' you had a little while ago. I see," Louise smiled. "Well, not to put it too crudely, has it occurred to you that this was just a way of getting out of any entanglement with you two? I mean they might of regretted having let it go this far."

"There probably is something in their contract about getting too familiar with the students. Young girl going loopy about horses, and then falling for the groom is not all that an unfamiliar cliché, is it?"

"I agree," I said. "But on the other hand, both boys seemed deadly serious, and I think it would have been out of character for them to devise such a roundabout way of crying off. After all, they only had to tell us that they had to be careful because of their positions in the school and that perhaps we should cool it for a bit. I mean there was no hint that any of us was taking this too seriously. Each of us has a steady partner so there was no great humiliation or pathological attachment involved. It was far too OTT and melodramatic, oddly enough, not to be genuine."

"Actually, I think you're right," Twinky said. "The whole thing seems genuine enough. I wonder how the message was conveyed to them. Was it in person or note through the door?"

"A brick through the window seems the likeliest," said Louise.

"Tell you what," said Twinky, "see if you can find out how they came to get the message. Gently, you know, quietly and friendly like and sorrowful for having seduced them into this precarious position. Want to make it up to them, sort of thing. All your fault, sort of attitude, if you see what I mean. Will you actually go riding tomorrow?"

I raised my eyebrows at Alice. "Well," she began, slowly, "We hadn't really decided whether or not to go. In fact, it hasn't so far occurred to us to make a decision either way, I don't know why. Probably we've just been too busy to think any further about it."

"Listen," said Louise. "That is an extremely good thought. Just be polite and non-committal tomorrow and if you have the opportunity of getting either one or both alone for a moment, just pop the question - sideways like. Slip it in - "

"Sort of in between the gap, as the actress said to the bishop,"

We all fell about sniggering and chortling and generally making idiots of ourselves. Twinky went up to the bar for another round of drinks.

"Louise is having a Perrier as she's driving," Twinky stated as she returned with a tray laden with nuts and crisps and drinks.

"We should be paying for this," said Alice. "I really feel a bit guilty. You've been such a help to us." She gave Twinky a hug and I gave Louise a hug and we were all very happy with each other, which is a good way to be with one's friends.

As Louise drove us home we spontaneously started singing. First off was the quartermaster's stores song. Alice and I had learnt the words while at secondary because for a time there was a phase of learning all the old naughty songs from early comedy films, which had swept like wildfire through the school, culminating in a spontaneous performance of the quartermaster's rat-infested stores to the intense embarrassment of our lovely headmistress and the staff. Well, it had been an end of term parents' day; probably not the best occasion for such an outburst. (From then on such impromptu vocal outpourings had been banned). Louise dropped us off back at the school; not being a boarder she went to her own home. Twinky had a room on the floor below ours. As we approached the front door she shyly asked us if she could have a sleepover as she was still rather wound up from the evening's fun-time. We were both only too happy to oblige her. After all, we had both been thinking the same thing ever since she had told what she thought of us. Well, that's hardly an offer one can refuse, is it?

* * *

Alice was the first to wake the following morning and she was already up and had put the kettle on - we had recently stocked up on some basic cooking equipment which was well hidden in the wardrobe and just brought out for specific use. I was still fairly somnolent as we hadn't got to sleep until about 3.00, a third person in bed with us being a new experience as it was apparently a new experience for Twink to wake up to two new companions in the bed she was sleeping in. Well, sleeping being a euphemism as not much sleep was taken that night! In fact Twinky, her little hand still active, was fully engaged to my continued satisfaction. Alice came and sat on the bed to watch this performance for a few moments. Then, manoeuvring herself between us, she encouraged us both most thoroughly in our pleasures. I think it true to say that we all enjoyed a very happy outcome that set us up nicely for the day ahead.

"Guys," said a little voice shyly from the entangled limb arrangements, "Aren't you going to riding this morning? It's half seven already."

Alice smacked a kiss on Twinky's lovely little face and bounced off the mattress. "Kettle's boiled," she said, "and tea is go!" She turned on the taps in the sink and gave herself a quick rubdown with the damp flannel, Afterwards throwing it straight into my face - which happened to have wandered down to the part of Twinky which she had abandoned moments before.

I also leapt - well, scrambled, - out of my little friend's embrace and rinsing the flannel under the tap did my ablutions. We both get dressed in double quick time, jodhpurs and all, including riding helmets & whips. Proper little madams, us.

"Twinky darling, stay or go as you please. See you later likewise. Don't do anything we wouldn't do without you and we should be back in time for last breakfast unless the string goes for a long canter."

"Can I just stay here for a bit? I need some sleep."

"Whatever you like, dearest," I kissed her gently. "See you later." We ran for it.

* * *

We arrived at the stables in time to saddle up the remaining two horses. It was a full string of riders today and it depended whether there would be a second set of riders later as to how long this ride would last. We would see. As it happened another couple of girls arrived at the stables as we were leaving so it was obviously going to be a short session today.

We eventually had a canter but not too much of one as the animals would have to go out again with new riders shortly after we had finished our turn. The weather was not all that beautiful that morning. A damp cold drizzle was the general condition with the occasional burst of driving sleet-like rain. We were rather glad when it was over. The seductive thought of a nice warm little body waiting for us in a warm and inviting bed kept our spirits up remarkably well. In fact it probably contributed to the successful outcome of our intended investigation into the source of the warning the boys claimed to have received.

As we dismounted and led the horses into their stalls, Alice hung back with Harry and speaking very quietly together it was obvious from the small smile and imperceptible nod that she had got the information we needed.

"Not all of it though - yet, " she murmured to me as we left the stables after giving our animals a brisk rub-down, covering them with their blankets and giving them a pat and a kiss which was the ritual at the end of every session. We waved casually to the boys, both of whom had managed to keep a cool distance between us that morning.

"It was a voice on the other end of a 'phone line. The only piece of information is the time that the call was made and the office number here if anybody can trace the call that way. Not much to go on really, but I suppose the police could find out if they could be bothered." We got back in time for the last half-hour of late Saturday breakfast and we ran up the stairs to see if Twinky was up yet. She obviously was, but not in our room. The beds had been remade and everything was back in its proper place. A note had been left on the sink top. "10.30 a.m. Have gone for long bath," it read. "Meet you downstairs when you return."

"Intelligent and sensible," commented Alice. "Little treasure, really!"

"Treasure, certainly," I echoed. "Wonder what her real name is."

We went back downstairs. The breakfast things had all been cleared away, but there was still some coffee. We poured ourselves a cup each and sat down with Charlie and Gloria, the redheaded student we had first seen at our inauguration ceremony last year and who now tagged around after Charlie. She seemed rather a lonely sort of person. This was not very surprising as she hardly endeared herself with her constant criticism and carping attitude towards not only her fellow class-mates but the staff, the visiting teachers, the villagers, the government and probably the rest of the global population. She certainly did not approve of us.

"Hi Charlie," we said. "Hi Gloria. How you doing?"

Charlie smiled at us. Big-hearted Charlie. Possibly the only person on the planet, with the exception of Lucy Davison, for whom Gloria did not have a bad word. (Did you notice how I constructed that so that it didn't end with a preposition? Neat, huh!)

Gloria scowled and said nothing. We had obviously interrupted some agonising from Gloria which needed out, otherwise Gloria might implode taking the whole school and surrounding countryside down some black hole with her.

"Gloria, why don't you come down to the Horse and Cart with us one evening after class?" This is Alice setting Gloria up for some mischief of her own. It would be interesting to see how it worked out.

"The Horse and Cart? Whatever is that?" demanded Gloria, outraged. "Is this one of your silly jokes?"

"No Gloria," Alice put on her earnest face. "Truly, it was just a friendly suggestion. You might enjoy a change of scene, have a drink with some of your colleagues and meet some new people. They're all very respectable middle-class professionals down there and I'm sure you would get to know somebody who would, well - um - not exactly match up to your standards, because that would be asking a bit much in a small village like this, but at least have some interesting thing to converse about with you. Come on, I'm sure you would enjoy yourself," she wheedled.

Gloria looked even more outraged. "Are you suggesting that I accompany you to a public house? You know that those places are forbidden to minors and you are breaking the law by even considering such an idea."

"Gloria," I said patiently, "We are both eighteen years old and perfectly entitled to go into any public house we want. And younger people can also go in if accompanied by an adult, behave themselves, which I'm sure you would do - you are seventeen, aren't you? - and drink no alcoholic beverages."

"Well, I'm jolly well not going anywhere near that place, thank you very much." Stoutly said, that girl.

"Oh, thank God for that," Alice breathed a sigh of relief. "I seriously thought for one horrible moment you might have taken me up on that offer. Phew!" Much wiping of imaginary sweat off forehead and exhaling of pent-up breath.

"You really are a bit naughty, you know," Charlie said as Gloria stormed out of the room, head up and breathing fire from her nostrils. "Suppose I'd better go and cool her down. Don't want to find the poor creature's smoking remains lying about the corridors. So much extra work for the cleaners you know." Charlie waggled her fingers at us as she went after her unhappy friend.

"Why did you send her up like that?" I enquired. "You know what she's like about drink, pubs, men, all the things we enjoy. Why antagonise her?"

"Well, it was either that or us leaving in a hurry. I can see Twinks there hovering in the hall. She finds Gloria a bit much to cope with because she's always on her case about this, that and the other."

"And how do you know about all this?" I asked. At that moment Twinks walked into the room.

"Tell you later," murmured Alice. "Wondered where you had got to," she said.

Twinks seated herself where Gloria had been sitting. "I had to have a bath," she said. "A long, hot soak with Epsom salts and oodles of Olbas oil - thought I might have a cold coming on - sniffles and all that! Glad you got rid of Gloria. I find the poor creature very trying and I really can't be doing with trying people today. Saturday is my day off with trying people. What say we go to the Groom & Dragon for lunch? I'm starving and it's my treat."

Alice and I both protested but Twinks was adamant. She had had the most super night with us and she wanted to thank us for our 'whorespitality' as she put it. We agreed on condition that next time was on us and she could stay over tonight as well; that is if she would like to.

"Oh boy!" she said, "It's like Christmas and birthday all rolled into one. Heaven!" She beamed at us and we followed her to her car which was in one of the garages at the rear of the building. It was a snazzy little red sports model and Alice elected to sit lengthways on the cramped back seat.

"Where, or rather how, did you become Twinky?" I asked her as I settled in on the passenger side.

"Tell you over lunch," she replied and we were off. I think she must have covered the fifteen miles to the Groom & Dragon at an average speed of 55 mph. it was pretty good going as mostly it was winding country roads - well, lanes more often than not - and she didn't wear her brake-pads down very much in the process. All I can say was that it was an experience. Consequently we were somewhat shaky when we finally arrived.

"Don't worry," Twink said as we stumbled into the pub, "I was just showing off. I'll be a bit more sedate on the return journey. "No problem," said Alice. "Just slowly enough for me to collect the bits and pieces that fell off on the outward journey will do me fine." Twinky laughed and gave Alice a squeeze, which brought the colour back into her cheeks. The lunch menu was simple enough. There was a vegetarian option - Sicilian caponata and omelettes - steak or steak & kidney pudding for the carnivores - and skate for the pescatarians.

"This is really quite a classy menu," said Alice appreciatively. "If the cooking is good, then I don't think one would find such select dishes very easily anywhere else."

"Oh, it is," Twinky replied. "People come from miles around. The reason I drove so fast coming here was that if you're not seated before 12.00 the chances of getting a table are pretty poor. Sometimes it's booked out anyway and then you either wait to the fag end or go somewhere else which is not so easy to find round here. Also the cooking is superb. Not only that, it's always fresh and the kitchen has never seen a microwave oven."

The food was indeed excellent and when we had finished our main course the waitress suggested we might like to have our coffees and any dessert of our choice in the residents' lounge so as to leave the tables free for the next customers. We settled with our coffees and I reminded Twinky that she was going to tell us the origins of her nickname if that was OK with her.

"My parents," she said bluntly, "wanted a boy. That was my first mistake, if you please. The second was my size and the third, although perhaps I shouldn't say it, was my intelligence. In fact I was a grave disappointment to them. First off they called me Patrick. Patrick, mark you, not Patricia or Pat or 'Trish, but Patrick. They dressed me as a boy, they had my hair cut like a boy, they would have sent me to a boys only school if they could have, but they did the next best thing and sent me to a comprehensive - a fucking comprehensive if you please, - where the majority of the pupils were either ESN or just plain sociopaths. My first day there I got bullied and beaten up by a gang of these little mobsters. I think it was only two days after that that they debagged me. That was when they discovered I didn't have that wonderful attribute of male superiority and dominance which is known as a penis in legal and medical jurisprudence, and a cock, willie, schlong, whatever, in the vernacular." A degree of bitterness had crept into her voice which grew in intensity as she continued with her narrative.

"They carried me, naked and bruised, round the playground chanting: 'Patrick's lost his willie, Patrick's lost his cock. I wonder where it's gone, do you think it's fallen off?'"

Twinky went silent. She had gone cold and shivery. We were so appalled we couldn't move. I wanted to throw my arms round her and shower her with the kisses she seemed to have promised me before lunch, but I was powerless to move a muscle. Alice had gone as white as a sheet and the tears were pouring down her face in such profusion that I was suddenly transported mentally to the scene in Alice in Wonderland where Alice's tears form a pond and almost drown all the little creatures who live down the rabbit-hole. I think we must have stopped breathing because my head started to swim and I had to breathe quite deeply. Alice was desperately trying to stop from sobbing out loud. I know how she felt, but we all react in different ways. Twinky slowly came from whatever distant place she had been inhabiting. She put her arms round Alice and laid her head on Alice's shoulder. "Listen, it all happened a long time ago and I'm sorry if I upset you. It just sometimes catches up with me. Shall I tell you the outcome of all this?"

"Please, if you can bear to," I said. "Do you want to talk about it?"

"Oh yes, I haven't told anybody about this in any detail ever, though I did write it all down at one point. The psychiatrist I had when I got very depressed thought it might be a good idea, so I did. But I didn't show it to him as I stopped going to see him because he really was a bore. He just sat there for an hour - not a second longer, the bastard, - and raked in the money. I might as well have spoken to a brick wall. It was all the go in those days - call it treatment! Ha!"

"So what was the outcome of this appalling situation?" asked Alice drying her eyes and trying to look intelligent. "Sorry about the tears - couldn't stop myself" she mumbled.

""That's all right," Twinky gave her a hug. "Thank you for being so sympathetic, or do I mean empathetic? Anyway whatever you were being is OK by me, so there. Well," she continued firmly. "Next thing I remember is the headmaster and half the teaching staff rushing out of the building and rescuing me. I was by then making what sounded to me like a terrible racket with my yelling. I was of course screaming in pain and humiliation and rage. If I had had the strength and ability I would have torn those bastards into little pieces."

Twinky stopped speaking for a moment and the look in her eyes at that moment were utterly feral. I could well believe that, given the opportunity she would have done what she proclaimed.

"The teachers then laid into the hooligans, gave them what for and frog-marched them into the building where the headmaster apparently caned them, an unheard of proceeding in those days, because corporal punishment had been banned for ages before that and the little shits usually just got a reprimand if any teacher dared to go even that far. In the old days when my Dad - my new Dad, that is - went to school, if you even looked wrongly at a teacher, he said you'd get the cane.

Anyhow, they got some clothes for me - this time a skirt and knickers, which one of the teachers went out to buy for me personally. Then all the questioning began and they got it out of me, the way I had been brought up to be a boy. There was a terrible row and I was put into care. I didn't mind all that much and eventually I didn't miss my parents. Something wonderful happened to me because of that assault. All those ruffians got actually expelled and the police were called in and I was given to a dear old couple - well they seemed old to me at the time - who treated me so well that I actually realised what happiness was for the first time in my life."

"How old were you then," Alice asked her. "Oh, I was probably just about eleven. I must have been otherwise I wouldn't have been at secondary school, would I? Anyway my newly adopted parents, Janet & John, - (would you believe it?) - they asked me what name would I like to be called by and of course I was so buttoned up in those days that I couldn't think straight, let alone think of a new name for myself. So they said to me that I should take my time about it and when I came across a name which I felt good about they would have my name changed by deed poll."

"Can you do that? I thought you weren't allowed to change your given name, just your surname."

"Oh yes, you can call yourself anything you like and of any sex you prefer. Well, in the meantime they said to me, sort of half jokingly that if I agreed they would like to call me Twinkletoes because I had such dainty little feet and they thought I might turn out to be a ballet dancer. I think there was probably some frustrated ambition lurking behind the idea, but there was nothing really to complain about and if that was pleasing to them who was I to argue? I was actually quite tickled and became almost proud of it. Also the name seemed to stick and I never bothered to change it. As the girls school I was transferred to was miles away from Middlesbrough, my home town, as were my new parents, it was easy enough to sever all ties with my birth parents and that dreadful place I went to."

A thought occurred to me. "You couldn't have been long at that comprehensive, could you?"

"Oh no," said Twinky. "This all happened after I'd been there only a few days as I said. It just took them that long to mark me for an easy target for their buffoonery."

"Some buffoonery," remarked Alice. "Those little gangsters have probably grown up to be big gangsters now. Enforcers for some local Mafioso no doubt."

"No doubt indeed," she agreed. "You can see how I got to Twinky, can't you. At my new school the girls were all called by their surnames by the staff, but of course all the girls called each other by their Christian or nicknames. I had had mine changed to Wright by my new parents as that was their name and that suited me just fine. I never want to hear the name of Braddock again as long as I live."

"What a terrible thing to happen, you poor love, you," Alice hugged and kissed her. I wanted to do so too but it would have meant standing up and going round the table, which was not the sort of thing one does in public. One or two customers seemed to have sensed a bit of drama going on and were casting inquisitive eyes on us.

"So you see," she continued brightly, "Twinky is my real name and not a nickname, I'm actually registered as Twinkletoes Wright, believe it or don't, but I could show you my passport."

"But you'd have to kill us!" Alice and I said in unison. Lunch was rounded off with a bout of hysterical laughter. It seemed to be becoming a habit.

We decided to go for a short walk, the weather still being overcast and drizzly but we needed some fresh air in our lungs after all that emotion. Twinky then drove us back to the school - or homewards as we had got used to thinking of it. I curled myself up on the back seat, not the most comfortable of places to be when haring round country roads at high speed. I wasn't surprised that Alice had been a bit shaky when we arrived at the pub. However, I wasn't in for any such ordeal. In fact Twinky's driving was exceptional, just a steady 25 to 30 mph and then a modest 60 when we reached the main road. We decided to stop at a small café that she recommended for its cakes and sandwiches, which she knew would be open on a Sunday afternoon. She hardly said a word over tea but at the same time seemed relaxed and friendly - just not her usual chatty self. I think Alice and I were quite grateful for the peace in which to digest all she had told us. I was certainly intrigued by this bit of history coming to light, spontaneously as it did.

We had polished off a whole plate of homemade cream cakes and were busy wiping the remains of the sugary confections off our lips, when Twinky gave us some further background to her story.

"My birth parents were working class and had little money which is why I was put in the comprehensive in the first place,. They would never have considered a grammar school, which I suppose might have been an even worse fate for me. I might have been turned into a sex slave by monstrous grammar school kids, mightn't I?"

"I think they just might have taken you to matron to find out why your willie hadn't descended yet!" Alice remarked drily. "What happened with your foster parents? They sent you to a girls' school, you said. Was it a sort of posh school, uniforms and deportment classes and suchlike?"

"Just about. They have money, my Mum & Dad and I never think of them as foster parents because they gave me a new start in life and are the kindest, most generous people you can imagine. They're still alive and in their sixties. I hope they live forever."

A tear rolled down her face. Oh dear, I thought in my selfish way, I do hope those two aren't going off on a crying jag or we'll be here all night. This time I was sitting next to her so I put my arm round her which seemed to calm her down a bit.

"Sorry," she said sadly. "I don't know where all this is coming from. I thought I was done with that part of my life. Obviously I haven't done with it at all."

"It will probably always be with you," I said - reassuringly, I hope. "It just depends on how much you will accept of it and then it loses its power to hurt so much. You know the idea: embrace everything as a learning curve and the sun shines out of every orifice, or so they tell me."

She grinned, "Yeah, I know. At the same time all my energy seems to have fled. I just want to go and lie down and sleep for ever now." She sniffed. "Maybe I've got a cold coming on."

"More likely a case of the lachrymosis if you ask me," Alice said.

"Come on, we'll pay for this and then we can go home." She beckoned to the waitress. "Do you want to stay with us tonight? Because you're absolutely welcome but if you would prefer to go your own room - ?"

"Oh no. I do want to stay with you tonight, but - " her face fell. "Won't it be pretty miserable for you both with me just crying myself to sleep? I mean -" she faltered.

"Twinky, we want you where we can look after you and be there for you, so please stay with us and rest as much as you want." I gave a gentle little shake. "Come on, girl, we love you. You're our friend, and that's what friends are for."

* * *

Sometime later that same evening found the three of us in our room. Twinky was snoring away gently on the two mattress arrangement on the floor and we were catching up on some homework and seated at our desks at the windows when there was a soft tap on the door.

"Who is it?" Alice called quietly.

"It's me, Louise," came the reply through the door. "Can I come in for a mo?"

Alice went to the door and opened it a crack and peered out. Then she opened the door wider to let Louise in.

"Shush, she's asleep. It's been a bit exhausting for the poor girl today so we said we would look after her in case she needs company or tea or anything."

"Oh good," Louise whispered back.

"Come and sit," I said. " We've got a visitor's chair if you like."

"No, I'll squat thanks," Louise said, and squatted down beside the bed and gently stroked Twinky's sleek black-haired head. "What brought all this on, then?" she asked.

"Would you like some tea?" Alice asked her. Louise nodded her thanks. "I heard that you went to the Dragon for lunch and afterwards she seemed to get in a state and you were all howling with tears running down your cheeks and sobbing and rending your garments and wailing about the end of days, etc. I have my sources, you know."

"And pretty fucking inaccurate they are too, if I may say so," said Alice, handing our visitor a cup of tea. "Sugar?"

"To sweeten the pill?"

"For your tea, idiot!"

"No thanks, and yes. Not entirely inaccurate. Twinky did get a bit upset didn't she? What was it about? Look, Twinky is one of my closest friends. If she gets unwell or hurt I look after her - all four of us look after her, do you see?"

"Of course we understand and we're not being deliberately unhelpful or trying to conceal anything for any reasons of our own apart from the fact that we swore to Twinky that we wouldn't say a word to anybody about what she told us."

"You see," Alice amended, "She told us that she hadn't told anybody else about this and we must promise not to tell. I don't know what to say, except that we can't, without her permission, speak about it."

"It's OK." a sleepy little voice came from the bed, "I didn't mean you not to tell Louise or Beattie or the other two. It was just not to prattle to Charlie or Gloria or anybody – (yawn) - else. Can I go back to sleep please?"

Louise lent over and planted a kiss on top of her head. "You do that, my poppet,"

"As if we would!" said Alice. She smiled at Louise. "Well, anyway she seems to be recovering quite well. What say we move over to the end of the room and we'll tell you all about it."

CHAPTER VII

Alice

Louise left us after we had brought her up to date concerning what for us, anyway, were the revelations about Twinky's early years. I don't think they were in truth such a revelation to Louise but I wouldn't take a bet on it either way. After reassuring herself that her friend was fast asleep and in good hands, she kissed us both and left for her home. We went back to our homework. Twink slept on.

"I wonder who reported our post-prandial scene to Louise," I said as we got undressed for bed. It had just gone 9.00 but we were both fairly exhausted by then, what with the previous night's shenanigans and the emotion-filled day.

"Probably one of the staff," suggested Rachel. "Tell me, how did you know about Twink and Gloria? You seemed to know quite a bit more than I do about their relationship."

"Oh nothing really, just an impression I got that Gloria's got a sort of pash on Twinky and Twinks feels she's got to be a bit protective of her. I'm possibly totally wrong so please don't mention it to her, will you."

"Forgotten it already."

"Best way. Do you want the starboard side or the port side of Sleeping P.?"

"Can I have the centre aisle?"

"You may not and for that I shall have the port side,"

"Fair enough. Let's be careful not to wake, else she turn into giant frog."

"Hush up your mouth and perish the thought! Let us board the Good Ship 'Sweet Dreams' and set sail for the Land of Nod!"

"Biblical as well. Fancy!"

Rachel turned the lights out, but there was enough moonlight for us to climb carefully in beside our little treasure. I don't know if Rachel lay awake all night, but I went out like a light.

* * *

The weeks ploughed on, as they are accustomed to do when filled from morning to night with intense learning and much physical activity. We had little time or energy left at the end of the day for our own personal sporting life, so togetherness was a cuddle before sinking into sleep and some fairly erotic dreams which involved not only the boys, who had apparently acquired some ways of increasing the dimensions of their private parts to alarming and quite disproportionate sizes. Well, that was my recurring phantasy anyway. Rachel refused to share her incubi with me so I had to make do with what I had. Apart from Louise, Twinky and the two boys, Lucy Davison figured quite often as a sort of Earth Mother figure, albeit with markedly lubricious tendencies.

The Easter vacation was fast approaching; in fact it was just a couple more weeks before we would be home for a fortnight's break. I must confess I was looking forward to a change from the intense levels of concentration and memorizing which we were obliged to assimilate every day.

Alas for the best-laid plans! Rachel had a letter from her parents to say that they were going to be away over that period - holiday arrangements had been made months ago - but my dozy parents had failed to check with them before buzzing off to some outer reaches of civilisation in pursuit of some either ultra-rare or, most likely, mythical shrub that could only be found in a jungle swamp or at the top of the Andes or some similar impossible location. I adore my parents but there times when I could cheerfully throw the mother & father of gigantic hissy fits.

The result of this was that they had arranged with the school for us to stay where we were over the holiday break. Well, I suppose it could have been worse. At least we could have a good rest and take in a film or two if we could persuade anybody to take us into the nearest town - or not as the case might be. Rachel was quite happy about it and a few days later the Head told us that we had received another invitation from the prince for a cocktail party at a country house just beyond the village perimeter.

The holiday started at the end of the week before Easter week, which was during the second week of April, a fairly early Easter in fact. We were invited on the Saturday following Good Friday. Little innocents that we were, we had not the slightest inkling what had been arranged for us, nor that for some time afterwards we were going to be completely unaware of what had actually happened. We waved goodbyes to Louise, Twinky and their chums after the last class on the Friday evening and met with the headmistress as we were walking back to our rooms.

"You will of course be catered for and looked after during the break," Miss Davison informed us. "I will be here, also Cook and Matron and the usual skeleton staff so I hope you won't be too bored. If you want to go into town for a film or concert there is a very reliable taxi service locally. Just let me know when you want it so that I can ensure it will available for you. I shall be coming to this cocktail party and you will find this a useful experience. I believe there are one or two business colleagues of the prince attending, so I'm sure you will do your best for the school. Finance is sometimes hard to come by these days. We need sponsors and backers and investors just like any other business, as I'm sure you appreciate. The lessons devoted to business practices will have taught you that, I'm sure."

She wished us a very good evening and took herself off to her private domain - wherever that was.

"Why," Rachel asked me, "does she always talk to us like something out of a textbook? It's a bit like a robot and she has such a lovely voice too. Do you think we embarrass her or something?"

"Mmm, she does act decidedly awkwardly but I don't think it's just us. After all, her lessons are completely different. She's one hundred per cent alive and in the present when she's teaching, so it's probably a social thing, maybe a class thing."

"Yeah," Rachel agreed. "The class thing is so deeply embedded in this country that it's going to take a long time to get rid of it - if ever. Vivat the Old Girls' Network!"

* * *

The next day was bright and the sun was already warming the rooftops as we went down for breakfast. The relative silence in the dining room felt strange and I missed the hubbub of girlie chatter and the odours of porridge, tea and fresh young bodies swirling around us.

"Let's do some drawing and painting today, shall we," Rachel suggested. "I haven't had a paint-brush in my hand since I don't know when."

I agreed to that but only after we had had a good run and some of our old games in the surrounding countryside, activities we had really had no time for with our busy work schedule. We could at last get back into the habit of a pre-breakfast run every day. However, I was quite up for some artistic work as we both enjoy sketching and doing outdoor scenes. I was never so good at drawing people but Rachel had quite a gift for cartoon sketches of a milder sort of the Gerald Scarfe type. I did think we should show willing at the stables, though and in spite of Harry and Jim's reserves about our possible relationship, I thought that an offer of mucking out or taking the gees for a spin would be acceptable. We might also find out a bit more about the voice on the other end of the threatening 'phone call. Rachel agreed and we decided to go to the stables immediately after breakfast and volunteer ourselves for a bit of horse-time.

Bert was the only person in the stable yard as we approached. The stalls were all empty.

"They're out on exercise," he said rather gruffly. "Won't be back for an hour or so, but if you want you can muck out the stalls and help me clean up the yard." (This is merely a translation of a series of grunts, which are Bert's normal intercommunication with the outside world. The originals would be hard to reproduce in print and you wouldn't understand them anyway).

We thanked him and set to with a will. Mucking out isn't everybody's idea of a holiday pursuit but we enjoyed every moment with the horses and had no problems with it. We worked away and had got to the washing down the yard stage when we heard the string coming down the lane. Harry was leading them and Jim rode in the rear like some defender against possible rustlers.

"It has been known to happen," Harry said in reply to our comment. "Not everybody round here is what they seem."

And with that enigmatic comment they busied themselves with settling the animals into their freshly turned out stalls.

"Good job," muttered Jim when they had finished and presumably in respect of our morning's labours. "Thank you, kind sir," we curtsied prettily.

Bert had busied himself immediately he heard the return of the horses with making an enormous pot of tea and eventually handed us each a mug of heavily sugared tannin.

"About that telephone call," I murmured to Harry, "Which one of you actually took the call?"

"That was Jim," he muttered under his breath. "Don't let on to Bert about this for God's sake. He'll have kittens if he suspects there's anything going on between us. What do you want to know for, anyway?"

"Well," I said pointing to a clump of trees on the horizon and trying to look as if I was asking questions of an educational value so as to satisfy any onlooker, including Bert, who might have the idea I was either flirting or arranging an assignation with the stable boy. (Shades of Lady Chatterley always present in people's minds, I fear!)

" Just wondered what type of voice it was, so that I know whom we're dealing with, if you get my meaning."

Harry scowled at me. "Look, this is nothing to do with you, so don't go round turning up stones where you've no business to be or you might get yourselves hurt."

"Well, I appreciate your concern," I said, "But it does concern me that we are being threatened by someone unknown for no good reason and that you and Jim, whom we have taken quite a fancy to, are also being terrorised. Do you understand?"

Harry looked sulky. "Well, you'd better talk to Jim," he said and turned away. Jim sidled up. "It were an East End accent," he said. "'Heavy gangster type, you know the sort of thing."

"Not mid-Eastern or Pakistani or anything like that?"

Jim shook his head and slunk away. Rachel, who had been keeping Bert engaged in domestic chitchat - well, I assumed it was just that and not some variation on the chat-up line - caught my eye and we said farewell to the males and walked back to the main house.

"Jim took the call and reckoned it was an East End heavy who delivered the message."

"How odd it all is," Rachel said. "I wonder what the purpose is and just how are we involved?"

"Are we involved?"

"Well, yes: naturally. The boys have been warned off us. Not for their benefit but someone else's who doesn't want us to be associated with them. Why?"

"Why, indeed. Let's do a run and then some sketching"

And so we did. The weather remained pleasantly warm and sunny and we had an enjoyable time after our exercise making sketches and watercolours of the house and gardens. As the fair spring weather continued that week we made the most of it, having great long walks and runs in the surrounding countryside, usually taking a picnic lunch with us but occasionally stopping at an inn or tea-shop and just enjoyed ourselves as itinerant tourists with sketch-books and pencils at the ready for anything that caught our fancy. We also spent a bit of time preparing ourselves for the upcoming cocktail party. The Head had reminded us of this at breakfast on the Saturday, so we went over our small collection of dresses to decide which would be the most appropriate for the occasion.

"You know what," Rachel said. "I think these white dresses would go well for both of us. Makes us look like sisters don't they. I think we would look stunning. What do you think?"

"Yeah, I think we'd go over large in these 'ere smocks," I said flippantly. "Just like a couple of little angels or maybe lambs to the slaughter, who knows."

Many a true word gets spoken in jest, but my last bit of flippancy turned to be only too prophetic.

* * *

That was about the last thing that either of us remembered when we awoke in our own separate beds to what we thought was the following morning. At any rate it was daylight and one of the last things of which we had any recollection was getting the white dresses out of the wardrobe and spreading them out on the beds. I remembered making some remark about lambs to Rachel and then it went fuzzy. I lay looking at the ceiling wondering why I was in bed on my own and why I was feeling so sick. I sat up and my senses went out of kilter. I sat shakily on the edge of the bed, felt the nausea welling up inside me and just made it to the sink in time. Rachel stirred on her bed. I rinsed my mouth out and washed my face in cold water. I just stood there hanging on to the sink and shaking. Then I had another attack of vomiting. Rachel rolled over onto her front and grunted at me what sounded like, "Turn off that fucking hoover," before falling back into sleep. The vomiting had now changed to dry heaves. Painful, but marginally less unpleasant. I staggered over and sat on the edge of her bed.

"Rache," I croaked, "Wake up. Tell me all this is a bad dream. What did I drink last night? I feel awful."

"Go 'way, silly cow!" was the sympathetic response. "Furroff!"

I furredoff and sat disconsolately on my own bed. I got up, drank some water and was immediately sick again. This time I just sipped the water and got back into bed.

Some hours later I was woken by Rachel being violently sick and crying into the hand-basin. When the spasms had passed I got out of my bed and putting my arms around her tried to lead her back to her bed but she threw me off savagely. "Don't touch me," she snarled. "Just leave me alone."

This truly frightened me and I didn't know what to do. I got dressed - very slowly - in my usual T-shirt and jeans. As I was tying the laces on my gym-shoes the thought occurred to me that something was very wrong with this picture. Surely the last time I had been up and about I had been wearing my white dress, not casual garments. I opened the wardrobe. Nada! No white dresses. Dresses, mark you. Two white dresses. One for me, and one for the temporarily deranged Rachel. I turned to Rachel to tell her about the missing garments. She was just standing there with an indescribable expression on her face, staring at the mirror. Without any warning she picked up the visitor's chair and hurled it straight at the end wall. Glass flew in all directions and the noise was almost unbearable. I know I shrieked with the pain of it. It was a wonder we were not injured by the flying glass. The maddened creature just stood there staring into space. The whole house seemed to have been shocked into an unearthly silence. Where was everybody? I wondered. Surely that racket would have caused someone to come running. No startled yells or running footsteps, no alarm bells ringing.. Then it came back to me. Holiday time. Who was left? Ah, Matron. Was this the beginning of a Carry On film? - Probably just the beginning of a sensible course of action. Rachel was going to need some professional help. Even when somewhat squiffy after a night out I had never know her to be aggressive or shouty or even to have that feral red-eyed look with which she had repelled my advances. No, this was serious nurse time, I told myself. I took the poor creature gently by the arm and we made our way quietly out of the room and went in search of nurse - for fear of something worse, as Belloc so elegantly rhymed it. Rachel remained in this trance-like state and when we reached the Sanatorium she made for the nearest bed and immediately fell asleep. I pulled the sheet and light blanket over her and tucked her in as best I could.

Matron was in her little cubbyhole - when was she ever out of it? - I gently tapped on the door.

"Come in, dear, come in," she cried. "My, you do look rather shaken. Was it a good party then? I know just the thing for you. Now then," she took a closer look at me. Her manner became somewhat more professional. "Sit down here, will you for a moment. I'll give you something simple to revive you first, then you must tell me all about it. You've been throwing up, haven't you? Yes, no denying it, I can smell it on your breath. Here, rinse your mouth out first then I'll give you my very own pick-me-up and you can tell me what's been going on, because this isn't like you at all, you poor thing."

As you have probably realised the chances of even a perfectly fit person to get a word in edgeways were slender; in my present condition the chances were nil.

"And how is your lovely friend? I hope she's not in the same condition."

"Probably worse," I managed to get out, weakly. "She's been ill, stormed at me, and is now sleeping it off next door."

"You are a caution, both of you, aren't you," Matron chided kindly. She went out to have a look at her new patient. "She does not look at all at her best," Matron commented. "I suppose you two have been partying a bit too unwisely."

"I suppose," I admitted. "Though that doesn't account for why I feel as if I had eaten about three dozen tainted oysters and washed them down with a glass of hemlock. Oh God, I'm going to be sick again!"

Matron got me to her hand-basin just in time and I spewed up what I thought was possibly the last of my stomach and intestines as well. I was crying with the pain of it.

"Christ!" I swore, "I can't stand this any more."

"Shush now, dearie. Now lovey, you just lie down on this nice bed next to your friend, and I'm going to give you a little pinprick. There, now, off you go to sleepy-byes and I'll have a look at Rachel and see what I can do for her."

Well, I'm assuming that that was roughly what she was prattling on about as I faded out of the picture.

When I regained consciousness, it was to find that I was again in a bed of someone else's choosing and dressed in a hospital nightshift. I had forgotten everything that had happened to me since waking up in our own room. This time it was in the San, the large dormitory-type of room, which was in Matron's charge. In the next bed Rachel lay on her side facing away from me. She wasn't snoring any longer. A third shape lay on the bed beyond Rachel. I tried to sit up and found I could manage it without feeling nauseous.

"Feeling a bit more yourself, lovey, are you?" Matron pattered over to me. "Do you feel up to coming in to my cubicle and telling me what you remember of the last two days?"

I nodded and got slowly out of the bed. I was feeling a bit more normal I had to admit, but my brain still felt sluggish. Something seemed odd about what Matron had just said to me.

"Last two days?" I asked. "You mean yesterday, don't you?"

"Well, dear. You went off with your friend and Miss Lucy - that's her in the bed the other side of your friend's bed - on Saturday evening just as it was getting dusk, and it's now just three minutes past five o'clock in the afternoon of Easter Monday, so I reckon that makes it two days, don't you?"

I settled myself in the patient's chair in the cubbyhole and Matron sat facing me. She looked very worried.

"Look, lovey," she said." Don't take this wrongly but I think there's more to this than just a hangover. I think you should let me examine you. I've had a peek at Rachel, and to be honest, with you as well when I got you into a nightdress and tucked you both up in your beds. If I was put in the dock at the Old Bailey I would have to confess that I think you had both been interfered with. Now, don't take on about it, just tell me if you feel anything unusual or unpleasant in your private area. The Headmistress also visited me while you were both asleep. She was feeling very out of sorts as well."

I stared at her, my mouth hanging open and most likely an expression of utter imbecility on my face. I slowly digested what she was saying and standing up I turned my back, pulled the hospital nightshift which Matron had dressed me in, and had a look at my crotch.

"There's a mirror over there," Matron's dispassionate voice came from behind me. "Just check yourself over."

I looked at myself in the mirror and, touching the area around my pubic bone must have connected with a tender spot for it made me jump. I explored a bit further and realised that I was in fact feeling very bruised and uncomfortable. I almost fainted on the spot because a wave of pain suddenly engulfed my whole pelvic area.

It was a burning pain that felt as if my womb and all it's attendant parts were on fire. Matron came over quickly and helped me back to the chair.

"I don't think there's much doubt, do you, Alice," she said. "I recommend that you let me examine you properly on the examination table and allow me to take samples from you. This -" she held up her hand to stop my protests, "This is basically for health reasons to make sure you have not come in contact with any disease, because that might ruin your chances of having healthy children or even any children. The sooner these infections are caught and treated the better all round as you know." I nodded acquiescence. She was perfectly right of course. It wasn't the examination that worried me, but the fact that I had been violated as had Rachel and for all I knew, so had Lucy Davison. But they were still fast asleep. I also knew that the sooner a swab was taken and samples sent for analysis the more accurate would be the diagnosis. Matron drew the curtains of the cubbyhole so that we were screened from any prying eyes. I got up on the table and Matron put a pillow behind my head.

"Now, dearie, I shall be as gentle as possible but I may just touch on a raw place. All I want for you to do if you can is to let me know as silently as possible because I don't want to disturb those two until I have to, and if they hear you bawling your head off in here it's not going to encourage them to follow your example, is it?"

I managed a feeble grin, "I'll be as good as gold, Nurse. I promise."

"That's my lovely girl," Matron drew on a pair of surgical gloves and started her examination. She caught me a couple of times but not badly. She was incredibly gentle and I realised what a professional she was. Nothing but the best for the Young Ladies Academy for Further Education, long may it last. I could feel her gently probing fingers opening up my vagina. She then took what appeared to be a speculum and an ophthalmoscope from a shelf and peered through it at my interior. She then got me to turn over and gave me a rectal examination. In spite of her gentle probing I couldn't avoid grunting when an absolutely horrible feeling of alien emptiness swept over me as her fingers touched some raw and sensitive place.

"Not nice is it, my love," she said sympathetically. "Finished here and now if you would be kind enough to raise your nightgown I should like to see whether you have any other bruising on your body."

I did as she asked. I was beginning to be aware of odd aches and pains coming from all areas of my body and they were becoming more acute with every passing minute.

"Why am I just beginning to feel all this pain?" I asked. "I feel as I've been badly beaten up."

She finished her examination and made a few notes in her note-pad. She had also taken some photographs of my pelvic area during the procedure and she took a few more of my back and breast area. At last she was finished. She hadn't taken all that long but with the increasing pain it seemed as if it taken about an hour. I glanced at the wall-clock and was amazed to find that the whole process was over in about twenty minutes.

I stood up off the table and let my nightgown fall around me.

"Are you in bearable pain, or is it getting worse?"

"Maybe it's my imagination," I replied, shivering, "but I really think it's getting much worse, and I think I'm going to faint if it goes on like this. Sorry to be such a wet, but - " I was almost sobbing with the pain. Matron gave me an injection in the thigh. The needle stung quite sharply.

"Sorry about that, but by the time I'd sprayed an anaesthetic to lessen the morphine injection, you might have had your fainting fit. Just sit down and breathe deeply and steadily and if you have a favourite mantra, repeat it so yourself. Here's some water for you." She handed me a glass of water. I hoped the morphine was going to kick in asap - I didn't feel any too brave or clever at that particular moment.

Matron settled back in her chair. "The reason that you are being flooded with pain is probably because whoever drugged you used a codeine derivative so that you didn't feel any pain from the abuse you were actually suffering and therefore you would not have struggled so much. It would also contribute to your amnesia. I just hope it wasn't Krokodil," she added under her breath, but I had heard what she said. "What is Krokodil?" I asked her. She apologised and said that I was not supposed to have heard that but as I had she told me that it was a particularly nasty form of codeine mixed with petrol and other unpleasantnesses which was very addictive. However, she thought that there wasn't too much risk of my getting hooked on it or anything else.

"Now, Alice, " she said firmly. "Your occupation for the next few days is going to be recovering as much as you can from your memory banks. It's all there somewhere in your head and you must do your best to access it, do you understand?"

"Oh yes, " I said coldly. "I'm of the same mind as you are and I'm sure Rachel and the headmistress will be as well. I'm going to find out who did this to my friend and Lucy Davison, if the same thing happened to her, which I pray did not, but I think it more likely that it did. We are going to find the culprits and then we will see what to do about them."

The woman opposite me seemed to have transmogrified very subtly into another personality. The new Matron was no longer the warm cuddly person whom I had come to see earlier in the day and whom I had seen sitting in her cubicle and smiling out on the world. Here was a cool, sharp mind with a spine of steel.

"Were you in the police or the army or something?" I asked curiously.

She smiled. "I worked as the medical examiner for the Forensic Office before I retired. I loved the work but I then got married and we lived in Kenya for a short time. Unfortunately my husband, who was a park ranger out there, was killed by poachers and I decided I'd had enough and came back home. This post was on offer so I took it. I had had enough of sudden death and relished the thought of a cosy little position in the country at a nice girls' school with measles as probably my biggest challenge. But there, human nature leads us a merry dance, does it not?" She smiled brightly and totally mischievously. In spite of myself, I couldn't resist grinning. I realised I was beginning to feel a bit more comfortable and the pain was receding satisfactorily.

"Now," said Matron. She opened a drawer of her desk and withdrew a notepad and handed it to me with a biro from the top of her desk. "You can either stay here or go back to your room, whichever you prefer. I would suggest you stay, as you will be there when your friend Rachel recovers consciousness and will be glad of your company, no doubt. Well, if not then you have the option to go back to your room. The headmistress I think will take much longer to recover as I consider her to have had a more severe shock, owing to age and circumstances, than you two young people. I by no means," she held up a hand, "am belittling the shock and outrage you feel and Rachel will also feel when she is awake enough to take this all on board, but Lucy Davison has to bear the further onus of responsibility to the school, her pupils, (you and Rachel), and also the Prince and in all probability is going to feel guilty at having put you in harm's way, although she is patently innocent of any collusion in this horrid business. Go and rest, child," she said. "I'll make some tea. Are you hungry by any chance?"

Suddenly I realised I was starving. "Oh God yes," I exclaimed. "But will my stomach keep it down?"

"A very sensible question. I'll start you with some soup and a little bread and see how we go. I'll just have a look at Rachel and see how she's doing. I think she will probably wake soon and I imagine she will be in the same state that you were, so that will facilitate my examination. But one can never take anything for granted - ever, can one!

Also," she added, "I'm going to start you on a course of antibiotics to take care of any complications. Have you any intolerance to penicillin?"

I assured her that although I had only been prescribed amoxicillin once for a dental infection, I had shown no signs of negative reaction. I was also feeling a bit more normal now. The situation might be horrifying but at least we had some stout professional support for our recovery.

CHAPTER VIII

Lucy Davison

It was with some mental confusion that I slowly regained consciousness and found myself lying on a hospital bed dressed in an unfamiliar smock-like garment which I took to be a nightgown of some official description. My first thought was that I had been in a traffic accident. I gently explored my body in search of medical appliances such as splints or bandages. None of these seemed to be present so I cautiously moved various parts of my anatomy in order to ascertain their functioning capabilities. Someone in a nurse's uniform leaned over me and asked me something. I couldn't make out what she was saying, although there was certainly something very familiar about her.

I'm afraid I must have appeared rather foolish as I just stared back at her without making any reply. I then tried to speak, and I think some commonplace inanity issued from my lips, perchance a demand to know where I was. How foolish one can be when faced with the unknown. I knew perfectly well where I was. I was lying in a bed in a hospital or nursing-home ward and I felt rather unwell, but I had no telltale aches or pains, so presumably I was physically uninjured. My mental state was very confused however, and I wondered whether I was an elderly person suffering some form of dementia, or if I had had a cardiac arrest or a stroke. I prayed that that would not be the outcome of any diagnosis.

The nurse person was making reassuring noises at me and obviously trying to convey to me the idea that I should just relax and continue to lie there and take it easy - those very words having become a bit more intelligible the more she spoke to me. My reaction to being told to "take it easy" has never been favourable and I was somehow aware that my usual reaction was sharp and contradictory. In this case, unfortunately, I was unable to formulate my normal response. Most frustrating and

71

even more so when I found anything but the feeblest of movements beyond my abilities. I seemed to have temporarily - I prayed to the Holy Mother that it was not a permanency - lost almost all my power of movement. Was I paralysed? Had I had some form of seizure or fallen prey to some hideous alien disease, which took control of the central nervous system and would I be confined to a wheelchair and an iron lung for the rest of my days?

Some of the nurse-person's words were beginning to be comprehensible now. "Don't worry, " she kept repeating, "you will be fine. You've just had a nasty attack of food-poisoning and if you just rest quietly you will soon be your old self again."

There was some jabbering in the same vein, which led me to the metaphysical contemplation of whether I wanted, indeed, to be my old self again. In the midst of this internal dialogue concerning who I actually was and my desire, or the reverse, to take up my former personality and functions, I had the good fortune to pass into a deep and untroubled sleep.

* * *

When I regained consciousness for the second time, my mind was much clearer and I now recognised the nurse to be the school matron. It did not, however, explain why I was lying on this bed in the Sanatorium.

"Why," I demanded, and it came out loud and clear, "am I lying on this bed in the Sanatorium?"

The door to Matron's cubicle opened and Matron's head appeared round the doorpost. "Oh good, I hope you're feeling better, Headmistress. I've got another patient in here at the moment but I'll be with you in a minute. Will you be all right for about another five minutes? There's water by your bed if you want. Look here, I'll just pour you out a glass and sit you up if you would like me to."

Deciding not to correct her faulty syntax I assured her that I would indeed like to sit up and a glass of water would be most welcome.

She bustled over and got me settled. She peered directly into my eyes and seemed satisfied with what she saw. "Just give me a few moments and I'll be with you. You're perfectly safe now and no need to worry. There's a bedpan if you need it so please remain as still as possible until I can come and check you over. You've had a rather nasty shock I'm afraid, but don't worry yourself about it."

And so she fussed over me and, of course, I started worrying, but as there seemed no point in disobeying her instructions I found I was quite content to remain sitting up in my bed, sipping water and trying to tease out from my sleepy brain the reason

I might be here. I saw, with something of a shock, that I had not the slightest notion of how long this had been, - several hours, I imagined, - or where I had been previously. Now, what was I doing exactly? An idea that I was getting into a taxi or hired conveyance of some sort was the last conscious thought available to me so far. I was filling in the blank spaces concerning who and what I was. These were now perfectly clear in my mind. My name was Lucy Davison, Headmistress of the Advanced Academy for Young Ladies. I was forty-four years old, unmarried but engaged in a quite satisfactory arrangement with the patron of the school, the Prince of a Small Caliphate, and that I have one or two proclivities which have no place in the public domain. I have a handpicked staff of quite exceptional ability who tutor about eighty or so young girls and young ladies in all the subjects that are so egregiously neglected by the state educational system. That this system has always been a thorn in my side goes without saying. It is not that it is totally inept, but rather that it is not nearly comprehensive enough. But enough of this! No point in ruminating on past frustrations. Focus, Lucy Davison! Focus on where and what you were doing and then fill in the gap between your last thought and your present condition.

Putting my gloves on as I stepped out to the waiting vehicle - that was first memory to jump up from the mist. Two people were already seated in the car. A taxi perhaps, as one of them, yes, that would be Alice Darwin perched on the tip-up seat facing backwards so as to allow me to seat myself beside her friend Rachel Katz.

Well done, Lucy. I gave myself a little pat on the back, metaphorically speaking. Now then, these two girls, ah yes, excellent students both of them, charming and intelligent, delightful company and quite unashamed of their very physical relationship.

Hmm, I wonder why I'm getting a slight twinge of discomfort and embarrassment when I think of those two seemingly sublimely happy creatures. Perhaps it's because I have always been so secretive about my own clandestine affairs with other women and am actually rather shy and embarrassed when I meet them face-to-face. Do I lust after either or both of them? - No, of course not. They may be very beautiful but my tastes are for more mature women (and men), and there is never any suggestion of a liaison with either of them. No, it's probably -

Stop it, Lucy, you're wandering off again. Concentrate, you foolish person!

Now, I'm getting into the taxi and Alice pulls the door shut and we drive off. Do I see the driver's face? No. Do I know exactly where we are heading? No. Why do I not know? Ah, I have been informed that a car will pick us up at 6.15 and take us to a cocktail party followed by a weekend stay at a country house weekend packed with recitals by well-know musical ensembles. This had promised to be most entertaining and Salim had apparently arranged it for me especially, knowing my love of classical music. I thought his invitation to the two girls was very generous and that they would appreciate the recitals. Also, I had not seen the prince for some time and I was looking forward to seeing him again.

How was this message conveyed? By telephone from someone purporting to be his secretary? But I knew his secretary, an amiable young Oxford graduate called Stevenson. John Stevenson.

So who was this other person calling themselves - ah yes - entertainments manager, that was it. Introduced himself as Albert Dunready and had sent the invitation card first to me, and a few days later, the cards inviting the two girls. RSVP was to be returned to the entertainments office of the conglomerate enterprises of which Salim was CEO. Then had followed the telephone call by this same Albert Dunready to confirm that all three of us were going to attend. I had not seen the Prince since the tea party a few weeks ago. He would from time to time disappear on a business trip and be uncontactable until his return. He said that it would not be a good idea for our relationship to become public knowledge as his family members, etc. etc. - well I did not take offence at that. In fact I was in total accord with the sentiment. Our relationship was of nobody else's concern but ours and I had never told any of my family or friends of it either. Fond as I am of the Prince, I knew from the very first that this was a transitory experience for both of us, albeit a very pleasurable one. He was a tremendously kind and thoughtful lover, considerate, yet incredibly passionate, also good fun and witty with it ---

Concentrate, Lucy! Grrrrr!

We are in the taxi, bowling away down some country lanes. Surely we must have spent some time on a main road. I couldn't remember that before and of course the reason was that I was busy chatting with the girls.. Small talk, of course and I can't remember a single word so I did not notice which way the cab was driving. All I could see of the driver was his back covered by some grey coloured uniform jacket and topped by a peaked cap. Short black hair, almost a crew cut and darkish brown skin, possibly Indian or middle eastern.

So when and where did we arrive? Impression of steps leading up to front door of country style house; I did not recognise the house and I was sure I had never been to it before that evening. A room with some early guests, all male, but talking fairly quietly amongst themselves. Now, who is it that greets us? Ah yes, affable young white male, who says he is Albert. We've never met but he is manager of the entertainments division of the conglomerate. The Prince will be arriving soon - held up at the airport - sincere apologies to young ladies and myself - would we like a drink, there is fruit juice or herbal teas if we would prefer - a gin and it? – Certainly, Headmistress, and what for the young ladies? Alice is it, and you must be Rachel. Ah yes, here is Mohammad with your drinks. Let me introduce you to -

Well, to whom? Oh, I had forgotten, little cakes and other delicacies had been offered as well, so we all took one or two out of politeness and they all looked, I remember now, most delicious.

Yes, but I don't seem to be able to get past that point. Did I suddenly feel faint? Did I black out? Fall senseless to the ground? What on earth happened after that?

Matron finally opened the door and came across to my bed. She was followed by Rachel who looked very white and shaken, poor child. "Now, Miss Davison," Matron said, briskly. "How do you feel? Would you be up to coming over to my cubicle where we can be a bit more private, so we won't disturb our sleeping beauty there."

It was only then that I turned my head and saw that the third bed on my left was occupied and there, if I was not mistaken about the glorious and enviable head of golden hair, lay Alice Darwin. "Good Heavens," I said, "Is she all right?"

"Nothing to worry about," Matron said firmly. "I gave her a mild sleeping draught as she's had rather a bad upset."

With Matron's help I managed to wriggle myself into a standing position and made it as far as the cubicle without accident. Matron sat opposite me and took my pulse, seemed to smell my breath, (a most strange and unaccountable procedure), and then took my blood pressure.

"Apologies for the breath-smelling," Matron said, "but it can be quite revealing in some cases. Not this time, however. You see, I think you and the girls have been drugged and then hypnotised to encourage you to wipe all memory of the last two days from your minds."

"Two days!" I was flabbergasted. "But surely it was only yesterday that we got in the taxi to go to the cocktail party?"

"Not so, I'm afraid. That was Saturday and today it is fairly late on Monday evening. I think, if you don't mind, I must give you a full but brief examination to see whether or not you came to any harm while you were out of the picture as it were. And then I think I will have to tell you some of the inferences I have drawn from my review of the condition of the two girls and yourself."

How could I possibly refuse?

CHAPTER IX

Rachel

I was flying; I was on fire; literally! My bowels were burning, the searing flames shooting from my vagina and my back passage were propelling me like a super-charged turbojet up and away into the clouds and diving back through them at an incredible speed so that I would go driving down, down, down earthwards until I plummeted straight into the fires of hell, when I would then plough my way up to the sky and the stars again. A roller coaster of pain-fuelled hate and misery which kept me alive and vengefully triumphant. I was a Goddess; I was Kali; I was Lord Shiva, Destroyer of the World. I was Terror and Damnation and all things foul. I burnt and ravished the land and slaughtered the people!!

Then I woke, or rather thought I had woken. I was at the top of our staircase at home. My mother and father were downstairs in our living room, chatting away as they did. I called out to them in desperation. I needed help; I was in agony, but they just went on chatting and took no notice of me. I tried to go downstairs but my legs failed me and I crumpled into a heap on the landing at the top of the stairs.

The next thing I knew was that I was being shaken and I was actually in our tumble-dryer at home again but trapped inside it; I was being tumbled round and round the barrel which was getting hotter and hotter every moment - or was it getting colder? - I was so confused with the shaking and the pain I tried to cry out but found my mouth wouldn't open. I then had the most terrible sense of desperation and started to bang on the doors of the drier trying to force it open.

Suddenly it opened and I fell out on a flood of bloody water which immediately engulfed me. I cried out with the pain and then my eyes were finally open and I was back in the real world.

I had fallen off the hospital bed and landed on the floor beside Matron, who was kneeling over me and trying to help me to my feet. I realised that in my struggle to awaken I had had some sort of convulsion, which had precipitated me so violently and so suddenly out of the bed that Matron had been unable to prevent my fall.

She picked me up in her arms and carried me into her cubicle, which was some indication of her strength. I am by no means a lightweight.

She sat me down in a chair and after a quick look into my eyes and murmuring reassurances, gave me an injection.

"Just keep breathing as slowly and gently as possible," I heard her say. "It's all under control now and we'll have you up and about and right as rain in no time."

Dream on, I thought to myself., this is not going to go away any too soon. The pain, however, was receding, and the feeling that my thighs, genital and stomach areas were on fire slowly diminished and I gradually became more aware of my surroundings.

"How are you feeling, now?" Matron asked.

"Less painful, but still raging mad," I replied. "What happened to me? I really want to know." I said fiercely.

"Well, I have a pretty good idea, but don't you think it would be a good idea for me to examine you first, so that I can give you an opinion not just founded on conjecture?"

"Examine away. Do you want me on this operating table here?"

"It's not exactly an operating table, more an examination table." She was treating my surly bad temper with tact and patience and I wish I could have responded better, but my sense of outrage was overwhelming. I tried to get out of the chair but found my legs wouldn't work properly.

"God fuck it," I spat. "Why the freaking arseholes can't I get out of this chair?"

"Because you have been very weakened and are expending your energy on rage and not on dealing with your immediate condition, that's why. Now please, take a deep breath and concentrate on your arms and legs to help yourself out of your chair. I will assist you if you wish."

"All right, suppose you'd better." I was not, I owned, being exactly gracious! Matron helped me on to the examination table, put a pillow behind my head and covered me with a light blanket. "Now, Rachel," she said patiently. "If you can help me by just bringing your feet up a bit towards you so as to raise your knees, I'll be able to examine you more easily, all right?

"Now," she lifted the end of the blanket. "See if you can gently let your knees just easily separate so that I can have a good look; this won't take too long. "

"Why are you looking up my fanny?" I demanded rudely. "What's so great about my fanny, that's what I want to know. That's all anybody wants from me, isn't it?

Just my cunt to look up - looking up my cunt and my arsehole, that's all they want - "

And that's all I remember mumbling as I passed out again.

When I regained consciousness a bit later I was feeling rather sick. Matron had either finished her examination or had waited for me to recover. I gave her a somewhat feeble but apologetic smile. "Sorry about all that, " I said. "It wasn't meant for you, any of it. I just couldn't control it."

"Don't worry,' Matron was nodding wisely. "I understand completely and I have heard worse. Not much worse, admittedly, but I've never taken that sort of rage personally. Better out than in whichever way you look at it. You have quite a good turn of verbal abuse, you know, you might work on it a bit. Read Rabelais, he's a good source." She smiled at me. "But I expect you have," she added with a chuckle.

"I've dipped into it," I admitted. "I love all those lists of things."

"Can you sit up for me, do you think?"

"I imagine so, in fact I hope so," I said, struggling, "and you might let me have a bucket as I think I'm going to throw up again."

A basin appeared as by magic and I heaved away at with little result apart from a sudden increase in the chronic throbbing pain in my guts. "Oh Lord," I sobbed. "This is too much. It's hurting like buggery again."

"All right, my dear," She helped me swing my legs round so that I was sitting on the edge of the bed. "Now, if you can just lift your nightgown up I need to have a look-see for any bruising you may have suffered. Yes, I see," she said and took some snaps of my upper body with a small handheld camera. "Fine, that will do. Now let's get you back in your chair while I get you a nice warm cup of soup which I'm going to get Cook to prepare for you now. Sip it slowly and if you feel sick again, just let me know."

She telephoned down to Cook and then, settling back in her own chair, asked me what I had last remembered before waking in the infirmary. I thought about it and hesitantly said that what was clearest in my mind were the terrible nightmares I had experienced and also the deceptive stages of actually waking from them.

"Do you remember what you were doing before that?" she demanded. "What was your last memory from yesterday?"

"That's easy," I told her. "We were going to this cocktail party with the prince. Was there a car accident? Did the taxi crash or something? I don't remember anything about the party, so I suppose we didn't get to it." Matron looked thoughtful. "No," she said slowly. "You did get to the party but there was no car accident, at least that I'm aware of. You are going to have to search your mind very carefully for some clues as to what happened to you. You see, you went to the party on Saturday evening just after six o'clock and it is now Monday night at about the same time. Two whole days. Think about it. You are forgetting two whole days of your recent past. And this has happened not only to you, but to Alice and the headmistress as well."

"What do they say happened to us?" I asked her.

"Very little as yet, but I would like you if you can, to let me know what memories come to you without any prompting because that way you are more certain of having genuine recollections and not filling in the spaces with other people's ideas."

I saw the point of this well enough, but I was still very confused, in pain and exhausted and I told her so - politely and even apologetically this time. Cook knocked on the door and came in with a tureen of soup. Matron thanked her and ladled out a dish for me.

"I can at least tell you that you have had a very unpleasant and harmful experience and none of it has been either your fault or the fault of Alice or Miss Davison. Now, when you've finished your soup, I think you would probably like to have some sleep, wouldn't you?" I drank the soup while Matron prepared a bowl for Alice and the Head and took it over to them. Unfortunately it didn't allay any of my fears, and when Matron suggested I lay down and tried to get some more sleep I was suddenly terrified. "I can't go through that nightmare again," I sobbed, "It's too terrifying, I think I might die if I have to ever experience anything so awful again."

I found I was crying almost uncontrollably. Matron gently took my empty bowl, put it on her desk and cradled me in her arms whispering reassuring words. Her motherly embrace brought me a level of calmness and she told me that she was going to prescribe me a mild sleeping draught which would allow me to get a good rest, safe from any bogies or terrifying thoughts. And so she did and I had to be satisfied with that as she led me back to bed and the next I knew it was morning and I woke again in the San feeling a bit better about myself. I sat up in my bed and looking round found the Headmistress also sitting up with a cup of tea beside her while she composedly tackled the Times crossword puzzle. Alice was similarly engaged with the Guardian. Matron, seeing that I was finally awake, came over with tea and the Independent.

"For God's sake," I couldn't help myself exclaiming. "It's like an old folk's home in Eastbourne!"

"Have you ever been to Eastbourne?" Lucy Davison enquired. "No, please don't bother to answer that!"

So saying she went back to her crossword puzzle.

CHAPTER X

Lucy Davison

After a somewhat skimpy breakfast, we four convened in my office. Safe from prying eyes and eavesdroppers - not that I expected any of course and Cook, who had been sworn to secrecy concerning anything she might have conjectured about our physical or collective mental state, was the only other witness to our presence there that morning. A reliable person and an old friend; I had no misgivings about her discretion or her loyalty. Matron, or Mrs. Victoria Stokes, as she is known to her friends and colleagues in her previous calling, took charge of the meeting.

"I should like to just say that anything you say here in this room will be treated in complete confidence. I think we all know each other well enough by now and I hope the three of you have enough shared experience over the last weekend to have little or no inhibition about expressing your memories and feelings openly to each other and also to me. Please remember that I am under an obligation to respect your confidentiality and also your trust in what we are going to have to discuss. Narrating what little memory you may have at the moment to each other will hopefully trigger other memories and we shall arrive more quickly, I believe, at a complete recall of the events of the last three days. It will not be at all pleasant but some degree of helpful catharsis will be achieved if you are as open as possible to what may be just hazy images, feelings or physical discomforts. Lucy, perhaps you would be kind enough to tell us what you remember after getting into the taxi."

"Do you not think, Victoria, that I should maybe open with a brief account of the invitation?" I queried. She thought it a sensible idea which might stir up some memories. I recounted how I had received the three invitation cards for myself and the two girls and how that this had been followed up by a telephone call to confirm whether or not we would definitely be coming for the weekend. I had replied that we were very much looking forward to the promised musical weekend and to hearing the distinguished musicians presenting such delightful programmes.

I then moved on to getting into the taxi and finding that Alice had left the forward-facing seat for me and how I had not seen the driver's face at any time and had not noticed much about the journey as it had become quite dark by then and I was busy conversing with the girls.

I remembered walking up the steps of the country house, being ushered into a sort of withdrawing-room, served with a drink and tasting one of the little oriental *petit fours*, and then going completely blank. I would begin to come to consciousness from time to time, I couldn't remember how often; neither did I have any idea of the passage of time until I finally woke up in the sanatorium. I did have the impression though, that I had been injected once or twice and I am sure that I moaned and struggled in my sleep. I looked up to see three pairs of eyes intently following every word.

"I'm afraid," I said, "that I have not contributed much to this reconstruction, if that is what this is."

"Never mind," said Matron, "I can confirm, however that you do have a number of fresh needle-marks in your upper arm and that a blood test has showed that you had a high degree of opiates and opioids in your system. Very well, who wants now to speak of her memories?"

Alice volunteered. She recalled that both she and Rachel were somehow separated from me shortly after arrival by some sort of business of choosing which type of herbal tea they preferred. Alice said that she was being so dazzled by the enormous box of mixed teas to choose from which were kept in a small adjacent room. She also did not notice that she and Rachel had been skillfully separated from each other, and that she was alone in a little anteroom with, she thought, two men of Indian or Pakistani appearance. A steaming pot of tea had been offered to her to decide whether she liked the smell of it. No sooner had she taken a lungful of the sweet smelling concoction than she felt faint and tried to find a chair to sit down. She recollected that a pair of hands had somehow caught hold of her and were guiding her toward a door in the corner of the room and the door being opened for her and somebody whispering in her ear that she should just lie down for a moment until the faintness had passed. After that, nothing; except for some impressions of being lifted up, carried and shaken or pushed about somehow. However there seemed to no particular pattern to any of this activity.

Rachel's account tallied more or less exactly with Alice's narrative. She too had been presented with a steaming cup of tea and had been led into an anteroom and to a couch to lie down and "recover her senses" as a voice had suggested to her. It was only in her dreams, or rather nightmares, that she was getting some clue as to what had happened to her.

The physical evidence was, of course, overwhelming. Without doubt the two girls had been ravished by a number of different men, probably of Asian origin, and also seriously manhandled into the bargain. They both had bruises on their arms and legs; also what appeared to be pinch marks on their breasts and buttocks and teeth marks in any number of places. The sexual organs were bruised, as was the anus; the back of the neck also bore the indication of some person chewing on the nape.

It was a horrific attack made by possibly as many as twenty men, which would only be verified when the samples taken from the girls were forensically tested and the results returned.

Victoria read the preliminary report to us when we had finished with what little we could contribute of our recalling of the events. She explained that she was not doing this to shock us or from any morbid motives, but was of the opinion that the sooner we understood the seriousness of the situation and what was involved the sooner we could hope for a solution and resolution of the attack.

"You may not want to bring any of this to the front of your minds, but I think that the wisest course in situations such as this is to face up to the reality of the situation with all the courage you can bring to it and, terrifying and horrible although it is, it is wiser not to bury things anything deep in your mind otherwise it will regulate your life choices probably very negatively in the future. My advice to you is to bite the bullet and bring the truth up so that you can see it clearly; also it would be wise to accept your reactions to these events and remember at all times that you are good people and you have no need to let a victim mentality play havoc with your relationship with the rest of the world. There are millions of decent people in the world and there are a small percentage of psychopathic and sociopathic individuals who prey on the rest of us."

She said that the only thing that had happened to me was that I had been drugged - to keep me out of the way, presumably, and that the real targets of the attack were the two girls.

"At a first guess, I would think that the two girls were chosen because it was believed that they were virtually virgins - in the sense that they had not known any man. Somebody must have had their eye on them for some time. It had possibly started at that first tea party. Somebody had been so impressed with them, probably because of their dramatic entry, and there was some antagonism about what might be considered in some cultures as an almost outrageous and offensive flaunting of women in public. Also, naturally, there was a financial reward to be considered.

There have been reports for some time now of a ring of Middle Eastern men who have been grooming young girls for sex and for sale. It was more than possible that a large amount of money had changed hands for the privilege of being a participant in these unholy delights!"

This seemed to be the most likely explanation of the motives behind this outrage. The two young people were obviously very distressed at having the matter put so plainly to them, even though they obviously accepted the cogency of Victoria's analysis.

"I think it also probably quite likely," she added, "that you were mildly drugged by something in the air of the taxi itself. This would have induced a feeling of euphoria which would have dulled the critical edge of your faculties before you even entered the house."

This seemed to depress the girls even more and I had the rather sinking feeling that happens when presented by unpalatable facts. The girls were obviously too exhausted for any further investigations that morning and they asked to be excused. They both said that they would relish a long hot bath with some sweet-smelling bath salts and that they would then come down for a meal afterwards. Both Victoria and I thought this a good plan and the pair left my study. It seemed only a few moments later, in the middle of a further discussion I was having with Victoria, (or more accurately, Victoria was having with me) that the door burst open and two white-faced young people stumbled into the room. "Can you both come back with us to our room?" Alice managed to blurt out. "Something terrible has happened!"

We followed the two girls up the staircase and along the corridor to their room. The first thing I noticed was the remainder of the shattered mirror scattered all over the floor. Behind it I was surprised to see an expanse of darkness conveying the impression that there was a large empty space behind where the mirror had been and not the end wall of the room which I had naturally expected. A broom lay on the floor and a path had been cleared of the mirrored shards. Victoria walked into the void behind where the mirror had previously laid and, as my eyes accustomed themselves to the scene in front of me, I noticed that there was a a tripod placed in the centre of the space and on it what looked like a small black attaché case. I followed, rather gingerly it must be said, and as I drew nearer I saw that it was, in fact some sort of electronic device. As my eyes followed Victoria as she went into the darkness of the space behind the mirror I became aware of a very strange feeling engulfing my whole being. I seemed to be floating after Victoria's receding back and then that I was being swallowed up into the darkness beyond. At the same time I could hear a sort of high-pitched screaming sound and in the periphery of my vision I had the impression that the two girls, one on either side of me, were somehow swelling up like balloons and accompanying me at a breakneck speed towards a pitch-black vacuum. And that is the last thing I remembered before oblivion swept over me.

CHAPTER XI

Matron

I was somewhat startled by Lucy Davison's scream and turned round in time to see the two girls, one on either side of the headmistress, catching her as she collapsed. We managed to lay her on her back on the nearest bed, Rachel's I believe, and for me to make a quick check of her vital signs.

"I think she probably fainted because of the shock of seeing the mirror broken and also on account of an after-effect of the drugs she has been injected with." I said. "You two will also have to take it very easily for some time and be prepared for something like this to happen. She should recover fairly quickly. Ah, yes, the eyelids are fluttering. Come along, headmistress, your country needs you."

This got a wan little smile from Alice, but Rachel looked as if she were about to burst into tears. "Perhaps you two might help to sweep up this glass before anybody cuts their feet on it while I help the headmistress recover. You might also," I added, "tell me how the mirror came to be smashed."

"I threw a chair at it." Rachel muttered after a rather strained silence. She took hold of the broom and started to sweep the broken bits of glass towards the wall opposite her bed. Alice left the room and returned a moment or so later with a dustpan, another brush and a medium-sized cardboard box which she had evidently found in the service locker in the passage outside. This kept them occupied while I attended to Lucy. Her eyes opened and I could see the stress of acute anxiety in them.

"I'm going to take your headmistress back to the San while you tidy up here," I said. "And when you've finished would you please come along yourselves. Bring anything you might want with you as I think you should not stay in here until this place has been properly investigated and the mirror replaced."

I got Lucy to her feet and helped her along the corridor to the sanatorium. It was evident to me that the girls would also have to have an eye kept on them and that I would need some help with this. I settled Lucy back in her bed and made her a strong cup of tea. She had recovered enough by now and I left her sitting in the chair beside her bed sipping at the tea. I took the opportunity of making one or two telephone calls. The first was to Louise Marchant, one of the Fab Five as they were known to the other girls who, apart from having a friendly disposition was also a trainee nurse and a person of whose integrity I was assured. The other consideration was that her father was a somewhat mysterious presence in one of the more secretive departments of government. I was in need of some professional advice with this situation. I also thought that Twinky, the other girl from the group who had had a sleepover with Alice and Rachel might need to be told what had happened. I was going to leave that decision to Louise though as I was not at all certain it would be a good idea to bring her into this mess as well.

"I think," I said to Lucy, "that we need some time to sort this all out. The girls and staff will be back at the end of this week and that will not give us enough time to investigate this matter and also repair any of the damage."

Lucy got herself to her feet and placed the cup and saucer carefully onto the small cabinet by her bed.

"I have been thinking much the same thoughts," she said. "We will have to get in touch with everybody and state that we have measles or chicken pox, or better still, some unknown infection, and that the school is in quarantine until further notice. It's drastic, of course, and may have a deleterious effect on the future but there is no alternative. We must get this matter cleared up and these villains caught and the whole disgraceful affair kept from the public."

"Louise is on her way and she is asking her father if he will come as well. They will probably both be arriving fairly soon, so I hope the two girls will feel up to telling us what they know. I've met Louise's father and he is surprisingly easy to trust, so all being well I think he will give us good advice."

"Splendid," said Lucy. "Donald Marchant is an old friend so I think I will now get properly dressed. I think the girls should also get dressed; it will help their recovery, I'm sure."

I thought this an excellent idea and went back to their bedroom to help them with the clear up and get them ready for the visitors.

I was pleased to see that they had got on with sweeping up the glass and putting the room to rights. Neither of them had apparently ventured into the dark space behind the mirror. Stupidly I had not thought to bring a torch with me but I walked gingerly into the open space, my eyes adjusting to the gloom. The device on the tripod was, I believed, not functioning at the moment, and when I had thought about the matter for a moment or two, I suspected that it would not be used again. I had a strong feeling that it had accomplished whatever business it had had there and the results would be stored somewhere beyond reach at present. However, it was possible that the person or persons who placed the camera would come to collect it at some point. That might be an opportunity to gain some useful information about the people behind this business.

I told the girls to get dressed and go down for the meal that Cook was preparing for them as Louise was on her way and that somebody else might also arrive who would not only provide some insights into the matter but also some protection for them and the school. The bulk of the glass having now been swept up and deposited in the cardboard box, they both agreed to get dressed and return to the San with whatever nightclothes and other possessions they would like to have with them for the next few days. They both elected to pack all their belongings in their suitcases and therefore clear the room of all their possessions. It was obvious that they had no intention of returning to it in the foreseeable future.

And this is where I must hand over the narrative of this sorry business to others more involved with clearing up and dealing with the matter. It might also be worth mentioning that I had no notion at the time of the existence of the diaries that the two girls had kept since their arrival at the school. It is however evident, that they subsequently recorded nothing more after the trauma of their attack.

CHAPTER XII

Louise

My God, those two poor girls, and the Head! What a dreadful business. Immediately she caught sight of me Rachel burst into almost uncontrollable sobbing and threw herself into my arms. Over her heaving shoulder I could see Alice, sitting, white-faced but determinedly dry-eyed, on her bed in the San. The Head was quietly drinking tea and Matron was fussing away about something in her cubicle. Matron had given the gist of things to me over the phone and asked me to get in touch with my Dad and ask him along too. Fortunately, it being a Easter Monday, he had been at home when Matron had rung, otherwise it's about a seven-hour drive from his London office. His sergeant, who often stayed in the village over the weekends, was going to drive him over to the school shortly before taking him up to his office. I had come in my own car. Rachel was calming down a bit now and we went over to Alice and had a group hug. Lucy Davison gave me a bleak little smile. I think she wouldn't have minded a bit of a hug as well, but I hadn't the nerve so I did my best with what I thought of as a sympathetic smile - which probably came over as a self-satisfied smirk. Why am I such a coward sometimes? Anyway Matron saved the day by coming round with cups of tea for us all.

Honestly, this country and its tea addiction! Over the Channel we would have been knocking back the brandy or the schnapps, whatever. Actually, I think I prefer tea when I come to think of it - the alternatives can be a bit headachy making!

Well, there I was getting soaked to the skin by Rache in the final stages of her lachrymosity and being heated up by the two girls and just beginning to feel that it might be wise to create a little distance between us - as much on account of ventilation as any hormonal stirrings in my midriff - when Matron presented us with these cups of tea, which necessitated the use of both hands and conveniently separated us to a more seemly distance from each other. It occurred to me that on one or two occasions during our training sessions I had experienced a somewhat unprofessional feeling towards these two. I also suspected Twinky of going even further with them, but that was never actually confirmed! How was it, I wondered, that these perfectly nice and friendly girls, managed to give off such powerful waves of sexuality? I decided to put this firmly at the back of my mind as being one of life's imponderables and not worth pursuing at present.

Rachel had managed to get herself a bit more together by now and Matron was giving a "stiff-upper-lip and don't-let-them-beat-you" sort of lecture and the Head was keeping a very low profile; so low in fact, that I almost forgot she was there; so it was somewhat of a surprise to us all when she suddenly spoke.

"No, not a sudden outbreak of measles. I don't think that would work very well," she was evidently continuing an earlier conversation of which I knew nothing. "I think it would be best if we discovered a serious problem with the drains which necessitated some essential works. This would give some credence to the presence of a number of men carrying out renovations to the building. Well," she addressed us, "It is obvious surely that the entrance to the room behind the shattered mirror must be investigated and sealed off. Also, that the rest of the building must be searched for any other spy cameras which have been installed. In fact it is a wonder that they were not removed when the girls were returned to their room. They must," she continued, "have been placed there during the renovations."

"I think that would be the best solution," a voice came from the doorway. I was as startled as anybody at my father materialising so silently at the door. He moves like a ghost sometimes. Quite disturbing, really.

"Daddy!" I exclaimed, and went to greet him at the door. With my father was an earnest looking young man, his sergeant, Alan Baker, whom I had got to know and like over the years he has been with Dad.

"Hello, Daddy," I greeted him demurely. (No extravagant exhibitions of filial devotion from yours truly when on the job, as it were)! "You found your way all right, then!" I observed inanely.

"Fortunately my sergeant knows the district quite well and also the front door was open," my father replied. "Good afternoon, Lucy, I understand you have something of a problem here." My father bent down and kissed our headmistress with propriety on the cheek and then greeted Matron with a handshake. He turned towards the two girls and introduced himself and Alan to them.

My father and the Head were old friends and the main reason that I was at The Yvette Coleman School for Advanced Girls as us senior young ladies like it to be known. He looked at the two girls sitting forlornly on the bed.

"I am, as you have probably surmised, Louise's father and this is my sergeant, Alan Baker. I understand you two young ladies have had something of an ordeal," he said gravely. "I expect you are also wondering how I can be of help to you. I think that can be best explained by saying that I have resources at my disposal which enable me to investigate serious crimes against the person; any criminal activity that has a political motive is my speciality. Whether that is the case here is not clear at the moment, but if you can bring yourselves to trust me and my colleague I should be grateful if you would tell us what you remember of recent events."

My father has that enviable quality of inspiring confidence and trust, albeit with a slight air of pomposity, and it seemed that Alice, at least, felt reasonably at ease with the two men. Rachel had withdrawn into her shell again after her sobbing fit and was content to let Alice relate what she could remember of the past two days.

Daddy and Alan then went up to the girls' bedroom to inspect the scene there. I hadn't actually seen the room, but from what Alice had related, the discovery of the space behind what was obviously a two-way mirror must weigh heavily on their minds. When they returned, Daddy made a telephone call to his office and told us that a forensic team would be on its way and would be here early the following morning.

Rachel had by now come out of her shell and seemed to have pulled herself together enough to admit to having one or two flashbacks of the last two days. The two chaps were having a confab with Matron and also having a look, as far as I could see, at the photos of the examination that Matron had carried out on the three women. (Matron had given me a quick rundown on this before I had telephoned Dad).

In the meantime I had decided to ask the girls if they wanted me to 'phone Twinky and ask her along to help with the nursing rota, because it was evident that however well they were holding up now, the dead of night was not far away and the nightmares and the demons would soon be abroad. Lucy Davison had joined the huddle in Matron's cubicle so I had to wait until they all came back into the San to ask them - all of them, of course - whether we might get Twinky involved as relief nurse. Alice and Rachel were only too happy to have her along and I was glad to find that there seemed to be no sense of shame or guilt at their predicament which would have inhibited them from informing any of their friends about the attack.

Daddy, of course, wanted to know how reliable she was and whether she could be trusted to keep the affair strictly secret. I could vouch for Twinky on that score as we had been friends for more than five years and I knew that a rather flippant exterior concealed a very loyal and honest person.

"Absolutely," I said. "She would be the best of all the girls. And what's more, you have met her, Daddy; remember? She came to my birthday party last year. Small, dark, lively, pigtails, looks about twelve years old, great fun."

He said gravely that he did indeed remember her, and that she had managed to get through something approaching half a bottle of his twenty-year-old malt, and had then given a fair rendition of Judy Garland, accompanied by myself as Fred Astaire performing 'We're a Couple of Swells' which did not somehow recommend her to him as much of a character reference. "What about Charlie?" Alice suggested. "You know, in case Twink can't do it."

I shook my head. Charlie would have it all round the village in no time at all; no malice, but in my opinion she could never keep a secret even if her life depended on it. I added that just because Twinks was a talented comedienne did not invalidate her as a person of probity and reliability, nor did her ability to consume half a gallon of the hard stuff and then perform a music hall sketch of much brilliance without falling flat on her face. Although it must be said she did do so immediately afterwards!

"All right," my father agreed. "Just ask her to come here asap, but don't tell her what it's about over the 'phone. Make it as casual as possible but if you can inject a little urgency into the seemingly innocent request I think that would be advisable. Matron and you, Louise, will be able to cope perfectly well until tomorrow, but I think we must get on and let the staff and pupils and anybody else who might turn up know that we have a major building problem here and nobody is to return until further notice. I'll organise security and a search team as well as the forensic lot from my car-phone, while Miss Davison and Matron can share the task of getting in touch with staff and families. If we can't get in touch with everybody then we must have the entrances to the school grounds sealed. What about the villagers? Do they visit here? Are there any other staff here at the moment? Cook, I think you told me, is on the premises".

The Head verified this and assured Dad that she was trustworthy. "There is of course Bert and the two stable-lads who will be around somewhere though they never come into the school premises, but Bert has his own little flat above the stables, and the two lads live in the village."

"Right, we'll wander round and see whether we can catch them before SOCO arrives. If you can point us in the right direction, Matron, please."

My father and his colleague went in search of Bert and the stable-lads with Matron leading the way. The San seemed curiously empty after they left. It was like a theatre after the play is over and the audience has gone home and all that is left are the cleaners collecting the detritus of the patrons and wondering why the lazy buggers didn't take their rubbish home with them. I thought of sharing this with the two girls, but they had sunk into a vacuous state and it was obviously no time for airing thoughts while thinking. Lucy Davison had put the kettle on again and was waiting for it to boil. She had the strangest look on her face, and I was persuaded to sit quietly and shrink into my own little shell for a moment. I then remembered that I had promised to get in touch with Twinky, so I telephoned again, but there was still no reply.

* * *

Thirty minutes later Dad and Alan returned with the news that they had managed to have a brief conversation with Bert, convinced that getting information out of him was so reminiscent of trying to open an oyster with a toothpick that they had no worries about any leakage to the press or anybody else from that quarter. The boys had apparently not been at their digs and not being aware of their barn in the woods until Alice mentioned it, had not been seen by them. Alice also told my father how both the boys had been threatened to keep away from her and Rachel, a detail she had not remembered until now.

"All right," my father said. "I think we now need to try and work out why this elaborate attack was planned and to whom" - (the parent's punctilio in syntactical matters was most impressive - to me at any rate)! "it was ultimately directed. If it had been purely for the sake of satisfying the perverted lusts of a group of degenerates, it was an unnecessarily complicated and perilous procedure. The risk of retribution and discovery far outweighs the effort of such a staging, and the victims are, I am convinced, not only yourselves. I think you were targeted because you are in residence here in this finishing school, so either the school itself is the ultimate target or specific people connected with the school are the final end-game as it were."

He paused for a moment to let this sink in. Lucy Davison looked horrified and Alice and Rachel looked merely bewildered. Matron nodded as if she knew exactly what Daddy was driving at and I had the glimmerings of an idea.

"Do you think ultimately that it's the Prince who is most at risk?" I asked.

"Good girl," Daddy nodded encouragingly. "I think that is a distinct possibility. It's obviously not unpremeditated fun and games, but a well-planned and serious assault. As that is the case, I am going to ensure that none of this leaks out to the press and if by any mischance the perpetrators are intending to brute this abroad, D notices will be issued. I don't think we have much time in which to catch these people, but we'll do our best."

"But what do they intend to do next?" asked the Head. "I don't see how they can make this public without incriminating themselves.

"I'm afraid that I do see the distinct possibility that they will claim responsibility, just in the same way that all terrorists groups do, which is to create fear and justify their actions. In this case, I think the object would be to discredit the Prince and shut down this institution. There are unfortunately many fundamentalist religious fanatics who despise and fear women and think that they are only suitable for menial labour and producing children. The Prince has much political clout in his country. If he suffers humiliation he will lose face and his country will be at the mercy of the sort of thugs we would not wish on any nation."

My dad looked fairly grim and Alan Barker didn't look very happy either.

"From what you've told me already, they will have footage of Alice and Rachel and also probably plenty of film of both of you to all intents and purposes eagerly participating in the revels."

"Christ Almighty!" breathed Alice. She buried her face in her hands. Rachel, on the other hand, seemed to have drawn some strength from somewhere deep inside herself.

""Hey," she said, gently shaking her friend's shoulder, "We'll get the bastards before they can do any more damage."

"I'm glad you are taking all this so bravely, but you will have to leave most of the work to us, you know. "

"Oh I know," Rachel replied confidently. "I was just using the 'we' in the sense of all of us contributing to the cause."

"Good," my father agreed. "Your job will be to remember all you can about the people concerned, where it took place and anything else prior to last weekend that might be relevant; any incident or person you came across which might have seemed out of the normal."

"We'll do our best," said Alice. "It would be a good idea, I think, for whoever is attending to us while we sleep to make a note of any night-time ramblings. I expect there'll be plenty of them!" she added bitterly.

"Your first concern must be for your recovery," Alan spoke for the first time since the introductions had taken place. "Try not to harbour guilt feelings or self-blame for what happened because - um - " he hesitated and dried up.

"It's all right," Rachel reassured him. "I don't think either of us is going down that road. The only feelings I personally harbour are an overwhelming desire to get these people caught and put in prison - preferably for life."

For a moment nobody spoke; then Alice gave a deep sigh, and we all turned to look at her.

"That's the least I could wish them," she said bitterly.

* * *

"I will need to get in touch with His Highness," Dad was taking over the reins again. "He will have to be told what has happened. He may also be able to point us in the right direction for discovering who masterminded this affair. I think you had better start getting in touch with your staff and pupils now, also any other people who might come to the school, such as grocery deliveries and similar tradespeople. The SOCO team should be here first thing tomorrow and we can get busy on finding out how they managed to get the three of you back into your beds without attracting attention to themselves in the process. I expect that there is a concealed entrance to the room that you discovered which will tell its own story. There will also be car tracks and perhaps, if we are lucky, a sighting of the vehicle used, but I don't want to put the locals on the alert by asking too many questions, so we will have to be a bit canny there."

Dad turned to me. "Will you please telephone your friend to come and help with night watch duties and anything else the ladies might need in the way of moral support."

I rang Twinky again from Matron's office and this time she picked up the 'phone. She promised to be with us within an hour or so. Fortunately she didn't live too far away. She said she would bring some books and videos to keep us all entertained, which might or might not be a good idea in the circumstances but I wasn't going to argue with her about it. Meanwhile Dad and Alan were going to take turns doing guard duty tonight until the reinforcements arrived early next day. I helped Matron prepare a couple of rooms for them on the ground floor so that they could take turns in getting some rest.

CHAPTER XIII

Alice

Yes, I know, Matron said neither of us was going to write in our diaries any more. Well, she was wrong about that and we did not tell her. In fact we both kept these pages secure for some time after the events you have been reading about. In those days, believe it or not, we used to keep a handwritten journal of things which interested us. Nowadays society is so besotted with their little electronic devices that on every train, (certainly in the UK) everybody, but every single person of whatever age, sex or race, is fiddling about with a little gadget which they are fixated on as with the lover's gaze onto an object of hero-worship. Books, newspapers, magazines, other human beings have absolutely no interest for them. Their lovesick eyes are cast downwards onto their laps where lie the objects of their madness, their loving fingers sweep images across the face of their fetishes, and they are transfixed in the thralldom of their adoration. It's more than a religion, vastly superior to heroin or cocaine and infinitely more addictive than anything the world has ever before witnessed. Whether there is a cure or whether total annihilation is the only way out of the predicament is problematic. Personally I think it might herald the end of the human race, but then I don't own an iPhone, a blackberry, an iPad or even a Raspberry, so who am I to comment on the state of mankind? ('Back to the plot' as they say on the occasion of the narrator running off at the mouth about some private grievance). Back in the '80s there were no social networking sites, no Facebook, YouTube or MySpace, also no available porn sites, no way of using social media for uploading films of beheadings or other atrocities, such as young ladies of supposedly modest virtue indulging in sexual antics with each other and groups of Asian men. But there were videos and films which could be edited to make it look as if they were fully conscious and willing participants.

I don't intend to trouble my readers with any of the interminable scribblings concerning reviving memories and nightmares which accompanied our recovery over the next few weeks. They were scrawled down on many sheets of paper and provided much needed catharsis for both of us over the ensuing weeks. The speed of the investigation by Donald Marchant and his colleagues was most impressive, and the arrest of the whole gang was carried out and completed within a couple of days. The recovery of the film material was successful and prevented any copies being made or distributed. In fact the person editing the film was caught red-handed when a special task force broke into his apartment.

I think I am trying to avoid remembering those trying days while we waited first for the clinical results of the rape tests, and then the disturbed nights and imaginings until we had finally brought the events of that awful weekend to our conscious minds. One outcome was that for some considerable time neither Rachel nor myself could bear the smell of Indian food: I think you will be able to work that one out for yourself, dear reader.

Our recovery was greatly helped by the tireless compassion and generosity of Louise, Twinky, Matron and the other three girls who made up the Fab Five. They had been gradually worked into the caring team when the school had reopened; a mere two days later than scheduled. Our room with its hidden anteroom had been closed off completely and access to the hidden stairway sealed. After about three weeks in the sanatorium, when we felt able to go to sleep without somebody there to watch over us, we were given separate but adjacent rooms in another part of the building. The reason given for this was that a serious structural fault had been discovered and we had been obliged to move into single rooms, as there were no more doubles available. We had no desire to return to our violated sanctuary at that time.

This brings me to the matter of our relationship and how we felt about each other after this appalling incident. I think it is fairly common for women (and men) who have been raped, to find a marked change in the attitude of their families and in the case of their partners. Although Rachel and I had absolutely no hang-ups or animus against each other, we thought it hygienically sensible to avoid any possibility of cross-infection until such time as we were completely recovered. We were also still in some acute discomfort from the bruising and internal damage done to us by those people. Our condition was explained as being the result of an automobile accident, which had left us cut, bruised and shaken, but not in need of hospitalisation. Our parents still being abroad, it was not thought necessary to alarm them by telling them anything at all. We certainly didn't want them coming back in a panic and finding that there was absolutely nothing they could contribute.

We gradually got back into class work and after a couple of weeks we turned up at the stables with a view to having a gentle trot on the ponies, (which was about all we felt fit enough for), and also to renew acquaintance with Harry and Jim.

Bert and the boys had of course had been fully aware of the police involvement as they had been questioned about the threatening telephone call and firmly but politely ordered not to discuss the matter with anybody. Unfortunately this happened some twelve years before the 1471 service came on line, but it was still possible to trace a call if there was a relevant time available.

"So what's been going on then?" Jim was blunt. We prevaricated.

"Just some silly person playing silly buggers," Rachel said. "Unfortunately the cops were called in and they're taking it all a bit too seriously."

"What happened to you, though?" asked Harry anxiously. "You don't look all that well, if you don't mind me saying so."

"No, we're still a bit shaken up." I replied. "Some idiot ran into our taxi when we were on our way into town. Got a bit bruised and that, so had to rest up a bit for a couple of weeks. What we would like is a gentle stroll with the ponies if that's all right with you."

"Mm, don't think we could manage more than that," Rachel chipped in. "By the way, that telephone call you got? Forget it. You're allowed to speak to us again."

We all laughed - a bit awkwardly, it has to be said. I don't think anybody felt very much at ease with anybody else that day. We were obviously holding back on what had really happening and the boys were, I imagine, debating with themselves whether to accept our glib explanation or not. Bert gave a grunt of total disbelief and turned his backs on us. The lads got the ponies out of their stable and after one look at our weak-kneed efforts, gently took over the process of saddling them up for us.

"Sorry," I murmured. "It was a bit worse than we want to admit."

"It's OK," Harry said sympathetically. "You just take your time getting well again and enjoy the ride. We'll come with you just to keep an eye, you know."

We set off at a gentle pace but it was obvious we weren't in any state for more than about ten minutes and even a jog trot was out of the question. The boys helped us down off the ponies but even so we could not help wincing a bit. We were both stiff and cramped from our enforced idleness and the aftermath of painkillers and antibiotics. We were still in quite a parlous state. Rachel stood supporting herself by keeping her hands on her pony's back. I walked very carefully over to the bench-seat outside the stable's office and sat down wearily. Harry followed and sat down beside me.

"This was no road accident, was it," he said quietly. "What really happened?"

"Can't tell you, I'm afraid," I said calmly. "And if I could," I added, "I don't think I would. Not for a long time, that's for sure."

Harry was silent. I remember that I was most impressed by his silence. It seemed to me that, contrary to what some might consider a lack of sympathy, it showed an inherent strength of character and breeding which was immediately empathetic and intelligent. Where another might have pressed questions on me, or expressions of concern, even demands for enlightenment, Harry was just leaving the door open for any need I might have for him.

I took his hand. "Give us time," I said. "It's all a bit raw at the moment. Also it's been dealt with very satisfactorily and we won't have any more trouble."

"OK," He nodded, and got up. "You'll let us take you out for a drink some time?"

"Of course," I smiled at him. "We're not going anywhere."

I got to my feet slowly and collected Rachel. We made our slow and careful way back to the school.

"Is this what being old is like?" demanded Rachel, bitterly. "Aching all over and hardly able to move quicker than a snail."

"Yep," I replied blithely. "Make the most of it, kiddo. We'll soon be fit and young again and raring to go. We'll look back on these least few weeks as the best times of our lives, full of glories and adventures and aches and pains and crap. Such fun!"

"You are a very strange person, Miss Darwin."

I was cheered to notice that this was the first time I seen anything like a smile on the face of my dear friend. I gave her arm a gentle squeeze.

"Ow!" she yelled, "For fuck's sake, girl. That hurt!"

Almost back to normal, then.

* * *

This might be a good place to record what action Louise's father and his merry men (plus one rather surly WPC) took against these people and what had prompted the attack. It was organised, as we had suspected, by Bahir, the prince's cousin who, taking advantage of the refurbishment of the school, had set up the two-way mirror, the viewing room behind it and the hidden cameras of which a number were found not only in our room but some of the single rooms as well. Our room had been the only one with a full-length two-way mirror, but a number of the other rooms, including the headmistress's had been bugged. Louise's father thought that the cameras had been left in the secret room on purpose in order to intimidate us. The search teams found recordings of the prince's visits to the headmistress as well as the private goings-on (for want of a better description) in the single rooms. God alone knows what revelations they had expected from the erstwhile ballet-room but they must have felt they had struck gold with our performances in front of that all-embracing mirror. Six feet high and five feet wide and we had revelled in our reflections as we made love to each other with such passion and joy. Well, we were not going to have that besmirched by their malign voyeurism. I also hoped that the headmistress, the prince and all the others who had been spied upon would remain unaware of this violation of their privacy and that the tapes would be destroyed.

Louise, who gave us most of this information, her father being very understandably reticent, was not sure about this. Neither were we. The tapes are probably in an evidence locker buried somewhere in the depths of MI5 (or even 6, who knows?) and I wish happiness to anybody who views them. The same cannot be said of the tapes that had been taken during that awful weekend, as they would not have been finally edited and must reveal the sheer disgusting behaviour of those involved with the rape and ill treatment of two unconscious females.

The object of it all was indeed the humiliation and overthrow of the prince and his ruling house. Supporting as he did, education for women and a democratic regime, he was very unpopular with a number of elements in his own country, and even if the Taliban had not got going so successfully again until the next decade, there were many fundamentalist Sharia law advocates who supported opposition to the prince's regime.

The house where we had been taken lay in a secluded valley not far from the school. We had been misled into thinking it was further by a mixture of chemicals being piped into the interior of the cab and some round-the-houses driving by our taxicab driver/abductor. The English components of the conspiracy were a local bunch of small-time villains who had been paid very well for some fake phone calls, taxi services and keeping their mouths firmly shut; not that that had done them any good in the long run as they had received punitive sentences at a trial held in camera. Such was the relationship between the fourth estate and the government of the day that no whisper of scandal concerning the school ever gained the public attention. The foreign members of the gang were repatriated for the prince to deal with as he saw fit. I expect that they just disappeared somewhere in the Syrian Desert.

The house itself had been discovered in the state it had been left in by the unfortunate owners on their return from vacation. It lay in an isolated spot and the gang, having had information from a venal travel agent, had moved in the day before our arrival, and prepared the house for our welcome. The returning rightful owners had been so appalled at the filthy state of the bedrooms and the rest of the premises that, after telephoning the police, they had both had a complete breakdown. The house was now deserted and on the market at a very low price.

Lucy Davison, our gentle, kind headmistress was recovering steadily from the effect of the drugs and when the prince had dealt with the situation in his native land, he came to stay at the school and the Head recovered even more quickly over the coming weeks. Towards the end of that action-packed term, we had news of our parents' return to England and a rather strange event was experienced by Rachel, myself, Harry and Jim. Rachel is going to tell you all about it.

CHAPTER XIV

Rachel

O ur parents had arrived home just in time to welcome us back for the summer break. I think we were both looking forward to having a couple of lazy months swimming and idling about; reading, going to the cinema, walks in the countryside, picnics and in fact a nice, normal, undemanding life. No more long days packed with constant new information and the acquisition of potentially lethal skills. After the first couple of weeks of the Spring term, we had returned for our Friday evening sessions but on account of our injuries and still weakened physical state, these had been limited to first stage weapon training and target practice at the firing range in the converted cow-byre behind the kitchen. Only a select few of the students at the school knew about this latter facility and although we had both had some inkling of its existence, thanks to the heavy hints dropped by Charlie at the start of our residence, it was only after the attack that Beattie inducted us into this branch of weapon training. After all, we were not yet fit enough for being thrown about the gym, mats or no mats!

As Alice has mentioned, everybody was very supportive of us. Louise and her sister trainers, Twinky, Beattie, Janet and Chloe knew what had happened to us but they, as did Matron and the Head, let it be known that our taxi had been in collision with a lorry on a dark wet evening during the Easter break, and we had been badly shaken up and would be *hors de combat* probably until the end of that term. It had been a long and uncomfortable eight weeks and I think we were both glad it was coming to an end. I think the other girls were glad of it as well. It must have been quite a strain nursing us back to health. I think and hope we had behaved well, but there were the odd times when we would sort of freak out and the only real evidence we had of this was witnessing each other's behaviour. If my episodes were similar to

Alice's then I think that we didn't draw too much attention to ourselves. We were both unusually short-tempered and given to periods of vagary when we didn't understand what was being said, but any outbursts of hysterical weeping were over by the time the rest of the school returned and although we both had moments of soul-destroying misery, they became fewer and less violent as the days passed. Darling Twinky and Louise were our rocks over those first few weeks. They were there for us twenty-four hours a day and must have been exhausted by the time the summer holidays arrived. They didn't falter or complain for one moment. Friends like that are rare to come by and at the time I did not think we would ever be able to repay their kindness. However it did all balance out in the following years, but that is another story.

Came the day when we were to return home, and Alice got this insane idea that we should ask Harry and Jim whether we could take the horses for a ride and go as far as our homes. This was not such an impractical idea as the route was entirely possible by country lanes, bridle paths and only one short distance down a village street which was not very busy and we could walk the horses there without raising any comment. Our families did not live all that far from the school so it would only take us about an hour and a half at the most. We could pack whatever gear we wanted to take home with us for the holidays into saddle-bags - available from the stables - take the boys with us, introduce them to the parents, have a bite of lunch and then the boys could bring the gees back to the school! Wonderful idea! A Fun Day Outing for Distressed Gentlewomen Who Had Been Gang-banged by Naughty People.

Well, the boys seemed up for it when we put it to them on the Saturday preceding the end of term. Bert was OK about it too and the Head approved with the proviso that we were checked by Matron to make sure we were fit enough physically and balanced enough psychologically to make the journey. Matron examined both of us thoroughly on the Sunday and kept an eye on us during the following week with a final check-up on the morning of our departure. We passed muster well enough. Our aches and pains had almost entirely disappeared and although we were not quite fit enough for being hurled about the gym, it was not thought that an hour or so of dignified trotting through the countryside would do us any harm. And we had the two sturdy young men as protectors. What could possibly go wrong?

So we set off, first of all having telephoned our parents and asking them if they could provide lunch for four and to expect us some time around noon. Also if some feed and water for four horses could be provided and the paddock at the back of Alice's parent's house be made available for their convenience that would be great. Alice held the receiver a distance from her ear as a cascade of extraordinary vituperation issued from the earpiece. Alice's mother is the kindest and most generous of people at the same time being the drama queen of all drama queens. A sudden change in voice and the mellow tones of her husband suddenly interrupted the flow. "Only four horses, you say?" I heard him enquiring politely.

"Yes, Dad. Only four. They wouldn't allow us to bring the whole string," Alice told him sweetly. "Do ask Mama to calm herself. I'm sure she will do herself a mischief if she continues in this vein."

Her mother had evidently grabbed the 'phone again. "You are in for a bit of mischief yourself, young lady," Alice removed the phone to a safe distance away from her ear again and the rant continued much to Matron's and our amusement.

"All right, Mama dearest," Alice replied serenely. "We'll be with you about noon. By the way, hope you found the vegetable you were looking for. You must tell us all about your trip over lunch."

"Lunch?!!" screamed the voice at the other end. Alice returned the hand-piece to its cradle. "Oh dear," Matron wiped her eye. "I haven't had such a good laugh since I don't know when."

* * *

It was just past 11.00 by the time we had packed our saddlebags, chosen our mounts, saddled them up and said our goodbyes to Matron, the Head, Cook and Bert who were the only staff remaining except for the caretakers who had arrived earlier that morning to be given final instructions and contact numbers in case of emergency. All the other girls and staff had departed the previous afternoon many of them not to return the following school year. The Head had regained her equilibrium and her health thanks to the ministrations of Matron and affectionate support of the Prince, who thought it impolitic to be present at our farewell. In any case we had both been wined and dined in grand style the night before by him and some of his entourage at a very famous (and ridiculously priced) restaurant in a neighbouring county, as much as a peace offering for the bad behaviour of his cousin as part of our training to fit into high society. On our return in one of the Prince's limos, Alice turned to me and murmured that perhaps the next lesson would be held in a chippy to instruct us in the etiquette of slumming it with the hoi polloi. The Head, who was sitting opposite us, leant forward and rebuked us for whispering. Alice apologised and countered the rebuke by saying that she was just advising me that I had a smut on my nose. This misfired somewhat as it had obviously slipped her mind that our headmistress was an accomplished lip-reader. One too many glasses of wine, I imagine.

It was a fine summer morning and I think we were all looking forward to the ride homewards with our friendly guests. We had been getting on much better terms with the boys and although we had visited their barn on one or two occasions, we had merely sat around and talked and played cards and enjoyed ourselves with each other's company. Both boys were keen bridge players and we had played a bit with our parents, especially mine, on occasion, so we were not too unevenly matched. Contract bridge, like any other game, is what you make of it. We played mostly for fun and even when we played for money the stakes were never high enough to arouse any negative passions. Both Harry and Jim seemed to understand intuitively that this period in our lives was not one for fun and games under their homemade multicoloured quilt and seemed content enough to go with the flow.

We set off across the field leading through Copley Woods but not taking the turn-off to the barn. After the first eight miles or so we were in unknown territory, but Jim had an ordnance survey map and had appointed himself lead rider on our journey. Everything was going satisfactorily until we found ourselves on a track in an unfamiliar field and Jim with a puzzled look on his face.

"Wurrn't sposed ter be yere," he complained. "And where are we supposed to be?" Harry enquired. Jim pointed to a spot on the map and held it up for us all to see.

"Can't see that from back here," said Harry. "You're the navigator, so get on with the navigating."

Jim shrugged and set off again in the direction in which we had been going. At the end of the field was a farm gate which had been left open, presumably on account of their being no animals in the field. We passed through it and into a cart track where Jim chose to turn left. It led up a slight rise along the edge of another wooded area. We came to an opening in the trees and an inviting looking path on our right hand side which led into the woods. Jim consulted his map again while we waited patiently for him to make up his mind. "Reckon this un'll do us," he said and we turned into the woodland path. It was certainly very pretty amongst the trees. There were even some bluebells still scattered around owing to the late spring that year. After about half a mile the trees seemed to close in on us and the canopy of foliage increasingly obscured the light of the sun.

"Do you actually know where we are?" Alice asked of Jim.

"It'll come out right, you'll see," Jim didn't sound entirely confident, but without turning back, which as we all know, is the last thing any traveller wishes, we pressed on into the steadily increasing darkness.

"I really don't like this," I said. I was beginning to feel decidedly jittery, but Jim forged on without replying.

"It's OK," Harry said from behind, "I can see it's getting lighter. Probably there was a bit of cloud ahead which blotted out the sun for a bit. Look, you can see it's getting clearer."

The path had narrowed considerably during the last few yards and we appeared to be in some sort of tunnel with the trees packed much closer together than seemed entirely natural. I could still see Jim seated on his horse ahead of me and I was blindly following his lead when he seemed to melt into the path ahead. This was puzzling but I kept going and suddenly I came into a sort of clearing. The daylight here was very strange, a sort of orangey-yellow. Jim had slowed down almost to a halt and behind me Alice and then Harry appeared looking distinctly perplexed.

"Where the devil are we now?" demanded Harry. Jim said nothing but urged his horse towards what seemed to be the source of the light. We followed and came upon a scene which literally took our breath away.

Behind us lay the forest and the pathway over which we had travelled and here, facing us, was an almost unimaginable vista. An enormous expanse of sand lay before us with the shore of the sea in the far distance. The beach glistened in the weird light so that it was obvious that the tide had receded and perhaps was at its lowest ebb, but what drew our attention and mounting horror was the enormous sun, low in the sky, with its sister moon far to one side and even lower on the horizon. The light coming from it was the source of the orangey-yellow colour which flooded the landscape, and my scientific brain was telling me that it was a very old sun and approaching the time when it would become a red giant which would eventually engulf the earth.

Just by writing these words brings back the smell of the ancient sea, the gentle slough of ocean breeze and the sight of an enormous flying manta ray which glided silently over our heads as we sat paralysed by the shock of this revelation. Our mounts were evidently suffering some anxiety themselves and had started fretting and snorting and exhibiting all the signs of acute panic. How long we stayed hypnotised by this bewildering scene is anybody's guess, but one particularly violent bucking from the normally sedate Rosie on whom I was perched, and the four of us turned tail and fled from the scene. Somehow the horses found their way through to the other side of this temporal gateway and careered blindly back down the path through the forest, past the bluebells and arrived at the cart track where we had turned off only moments before. We were in such a state of shock that none of us could think straight, let alone speak, so it was as well that our mounts, who had managed to throw off their terror by their mad gallop, were now serenely trotting along as if nothing untoward had happened. As if we hadn't had a glimpse of some future - or past - world, in which we couldn't have survived for very long even if we hadn't probably been carried off by some giant flying monstrosity to feed its hungry offspring. Why did I have such a thought? Eventually we came upon the village with which Alice and I were very familiar. We dismounted and led the four animals, who by now were completely over their perturbation and calm and docile as usual. Lucky them, I thought. Wish I felt like that.

Strangely, none of us was willing to voice any of our feelings. I can only suppose that, like myself, they were in some state of shock and strangely enough I could see that there was in reality very little one could say about the matter.

We weren't going to go on the Terry Wogan Show or get ourselves interviewed by David Frost for relating a totally unbelievable incident that was, truly, totally unbelievable. In fact it was so unbelievable that we were reluctant to discuss it even amongst ourselves. Perhaps at some later date one of us might bring up the notion that something rather odd had happened to us in the woods that day - (Please, no Teddy Bear jokes!) - and we could then compare notes, but it was certainly no time to go blurting this out to anybody else or we would end up in the funny bin with a lot of psychiatrists, psychologists and just plain psychos drugging us out of our minds. So, by a sort of tacit consent we mentally pulled ourselves together so as to deal with my any queries from my own dear parents and Alice's dear but demented progenitors!

CHAPTER XV

Alice

Our house lay some hundred yards or so at the brow of a gentle incline of rough track which carried on into the neighbouring farmer's fields. Rachel's house was a quarter of a mile to the east and had a more sheltered position on the edge of some woodland. By road the distance between our two houses amounted to over three miles, by foot a twenty-minute walk for the average pedestrian. My father had been keeping a lookout for us, patient man that he is and, as we approached - Rachel and I were leading now we had reached our home territory - he beckoned to us to follow him through a side gate and into the paddock at the rear of the garden. We could see Rachel's parents setting up the garden table for an alfresco lunch. Dad had managed to find some hay for the gees and a disused bathtub was being filled from a garden hose clamped on to the rim of it. The family dogs, Bennie and Sully, (Doberman and Lurcher, our two lovely bullterriers having died a couple of years earlier), greeted us in their usual enthusiastic doggy fashion. We dismounted and we gave them a hug and then my Dad a hug and introduced him to Harry & Jim, who shook hands politely but were fairly silent. Well, I imagine all four of us felt a bit unreal after our experience of only half an hour ago. However I did manage to give my father a really affectionate greeting, as did Rachel. We said we would join the rest of the family in the garden as soon as we had seen to our steeds. My mother was most likely in the kitchen bossing the lunch around and creating her own little madness. We finished settling the horses and leaving them free to roam and graze in the security of the paddock we wandered through to the back garden.

Mum came out into the garden and Rachel and I gave her and her own parents a good old hug and introduced the boys. It was so good to see them all again, and when the greetings and introductions were over, Rachel's father provided us with some home-made lemonade for us and some home-made beer for the boys who politely refused it saying they were driving home afterwards. (Harry made this pleasantry; Jim just sort of smiled politely and remained his usual taciturn self). I should say here that this lack of conversation didn't seem to cast any sort of shadow over the gathering, rather the opposite in fact; I had the feeling that the best and safest course of the conversation would be one that flowed uninterruptedly through the quiet and placid reaches of observations concerning the weather, the lateness of the Spring, the local gossip about the neighbours and of course the beauty of the horses and how many there were at the school and were there many pupils who wanted to ride, etc.

And so it flowed on in a safely monotonous way and, as no alcohol had been taken, tempers remained calm and any of the burning questions which might possibly be lurking just beneath the bland, strangely static exteriors of our elders remained safely unspoken - for the time being anyway. I feared the irruptions that would inevitably follow Harry and Jim's departure, but short of jumping on our horses and careering off with them back from where we had come, I saw no alternative than to stay and face whatever discomforting times were to come. And it then occurred to me that I really had no cause for alarm. The experience that the four of us had had that morning had ultimately, once the terror had receded, left us in a state of utter tranquility as if we had now experienced something so profound that nothing could ever disturb or harm us. And, indeed when certain events happened later in our lives which should have given us great concern for our safety, we always had the memory of that extraordinary scene and could revisit that place in our minds, which saved us on many occasions from panicky actions which otherwise might have destroyed us. (You might wonder why I am speaking for each of us, but we did compare notes at a later date and reported almost the exact same knowledge of our own inner strengths which we had gained that morning). And so it was that the four of us, arriving with no tensions, social, sexual or otherwise, and calm and content in our own bodies, cast an atmosphere of tranquility over the company and allayed any worries or concerns that our parents might have had for our well-being.

I managed to catch Rachel's eye just as both our fathers handed round a portion of a truly delicious sherry trifle which they had concocted between them, my mother having cooked the first course of lamb stew for the carnivores; nut roast (a truly good dish when properly prepared) for Rachel and me, being the only vegetarians in the gathering. Rachel's mother, Rebecca, had done all the donkeywork of scrubbing the new potatoes and slicing up the vegetables while Vera, my bonkers earth mother, created! Rachel managed to signal back more or less telepathically, that we should treat any forthcoming interrogation with calm and not divulge anything further than what we had agreed upon that morning. Our cover story was that we had been run off the road while in a taxi on it's way to a recital in the nearest large town. We had already checked details and committed them to memory because, knowing my parents particularly, (Rachel's apparently, but deceptively, being much more trusting and innocent), we would not put it past them to check up on every last detail. I wasn't entirely sure why we had decided to be so cagey with them, but I think it was a mixture of embarrassment and concern that they would be: a) upset and overly concerned about us, b) that they might prevent us returning the following academic year and c) that it might inhibit their own needs to travel and explore the world. We had discussed this with the Head and Matron and also Louise, and as far as we were concerned there was no doubt in our minds that we wanted to continue at the school. For one thing we were having, in spite of the hard work, some of the best experiences of our lives and had made some truly lovely friends, met some very interesting people and had broadened our minds and vision of the world to the extent of never being able to return to the homely but narrow existence of previous years. Even the harrowing experience of two months ago had broadened our horizons immeasurably. There's nothing like a really bad event to strengthen one, as long as it doesn't destroy you, and neither of us was going to be destroyed by anything or anybody - that we had both resolved upon.

In the event, neither my parents nor Rachel's made any comment on our tale of dangerous driving in the countryside, but seemed to be quite content with our little fabrication. We decided later that, in spite of feeling a modicum of guilt about keeping the whole truth from them, we thought there were times when this was the better option. The burden would have been most unfair on them and would only have served the purpose designed by the perpetrators of the outrage that was to disturb and harm innocent people. Transparency is all very well, but there are definitely times when it is wiser and kinder not to reveal too much of the wickedness of the world. So, I hear you cry, why are we telling you this story? Well, it's pretty obvious, isn't it, that you have no idea who we are and are not connected to us in any way and it would be most unlikely that any of the persons on the periphery of this account would connect with the events of so long ago. That is why so much in public life is withheld from public scrutiny until at least thirty years have passed. Occasionally this confidentiality is abused, but that is the price to be paid for saving some very good people's reputations and also protecting the public from much anxiety and panic.

And so the lunch passed off very successfully, the food was delicious and much appreciated and the guests were made to feel like family members and were appreciated for their good looks and nice manners and pleasant conversation and all went off quite copacetically!

We waved the boys good-bye as they led the two spare horses back down the track outside our house, issuing an invitation to visit again if they had the time and inclination. Our parents made cooing noises about their suitability as our friends and hoped that we would invite them over again during the holidays. There was a slight suggestion that they would quite approve of them as acceptable boy friends for us if things developed further. My mum forbore to make any ribald comment about their attractiveness which was quite surprising really!

We helped clear up the lunch dishes and I did the washing up while Rachel dried. We took our belongings upstairs after we had finished replacing all the crockery, cutlery and cooking utensils in their proper places. The parents were sitting on the garden probably discussing us or maybe not, who knows?

We unpacked and Rachel went into the bathroom to have a wash and do her teeth, came back, finished undressing and got into bed. I then went to the bathroom and went through more or less the same ritual, came back to the bedroom, undressed and climbed into the bed beside her.

"Do you realise," I said, "that this is first time we have been in bed together for over eight weeks?"

"An unheard of and totally unacceptable state of affairs," Rachel observed. She laid her head on my shoulder. "You know, I'm still feeling a bit tender and uncomfortable," she added. "And that ride this morning has rather taken it out of me, Especially," she added. "that fast bit!"

"I know," I said. "Especially the fast bit." I stroked her face gently and planted a kiss on the side of her head. We just lay there, warm and comfortable with each other and glad to be together again and at peace with the world. And we dozed and woke and were gentle with each other and slept again until it grew dark outside and the moonlight came through the window and cast shadows, lovely and enchanting shadows full of promise of a good life ahead of us and our friends.

Thinking about it now, I can look back on that day and be aware that that was the beginning of a new stage in our lives. It was as if we had somehow passed some trial or exam with flying colours and been awarded the highest recognition for our achievement. And yet, what had we actually done? I felt that most if it had in fact, been done to us and not really by us. Did that matter? Well, not really. If one is chosen for a certain path it's probably better just to go with the flow and accept one's fate. I've come to the conclusion (well, a working conclusion, let's say) that the less resistance one puts up the more energy one has for enjoying whatever life has to offer. Ultimately the assault on us was nothing of our choosing or our responsibility. That started when we regained consciousness and made a decision on what we were going to do about it. The incident in the woods was a sign of something which, in our limited knowledge of how the universe works, we might never fully understand. Notwithstanding that, it was a most amazing and wonderful experience and led me to believe that it more than compensated for the indignity which we had sustained at the hands of a gang of vicious and unprincipled thugs.

EPILOGUE

Vera

When they left after Christmas to go back to Silverton, they were two (fairly) normal teenage girls with laughter and mischief in their eyes. They came back only six months later looking as if they had seen and experienced almost everything possible. The bonus was that they and their two young men were so easy to be with. They didn't seem to need to be entertained or to be needy in the usual way of teenagers nowadays, forever after instant gratification. It was a delightful day we had with them. The only drawback was that they seemed to have travelled further in those six months than any of us adults normally travel within six years.

I think I should explain a little concerning our particular place in their lives as their parents. Tom and I are botanists by profession but we use that as our cover for access to various parts of the world that would not normally be reachable. We gather information about the political and domestic situations in those areas we are allowed to visit. We also live with the constant danger of being unmasked and consequently being imprisoned or killed. Our friends and neighbours, Rebecca and Joseph Katz, were medical researchers who used their valuable knowledge to help out with institutions like *Medicens sans Frontiéres* wherever they could, and were also a useful source of information for the intelligence services. In fact, we were secret agents. I think Joseph and Rebecca ran an even greater risk than we did, but the point of telling you this is to explain how our daughters came to be in training at an institution which taught spy-craft and kindred subjects.

We had agreed after much discussion and some encouragement from our mentors in the Intelligence Service that not only had the two girls great potential for the work, but it was also safer in the long run to have them professionally equipped for trouble if, as might very well happen, we ran into danger at our homes. Dartmoor is a quiet and lovely area, but nowhere is safe from attack once the location is targeted. And so it was that H.M. Government kindly paid the enormous fees for the training at Silverton and, even if the girls did not sign up for service they would have had an extremely good education.

It might also be worth mentioning that immediately we had arrived back in England, (Tom and I had returned six days before Joseph & Rebecca) both Donald Marchant and Lucy Davison had brought us up to date with the situation regarding our daughters. We were, of course, appalled and Tom did have quite a job in restraining me from tearing off to Silverton and - well, I didn't know what was in my mind at that point. Some wild notion of rescuing our beautiful daughters - each set of parents regarded both girls as being their daughters! - from a fate worse than death or, preferably shooting someone, anyone who was available to be shot, I suppose!

Fortunately sense prevailed after the first rush of blood to my head. As my dear husband managed to instil in my fevered mind, the fate worse than death had already occurred, the girls were virtually recovered from the worst of the ordeal, all the perpetrators of the outrage were either banged up or had been taken care of by traditional middle eastern protocols, and there was nothing we could do for the girls but welcome them home when they arrived the following week, and let them tell their story in their own time; if that was what they wanted to do. As it turned out, they didn't want us to know the first thing about the attack, so we all went along with it and had a very good time together. Both our families are extremely accomplished at keeping secrets as you will have gathered, and although I think there was some sadness that Alice and Rachel were now leaving the nest, it was more than compensated by the realisation that they were rapidly blossoming into young womanhood with such a professional and accomplished air of maturity about them. We were also made fully aware that they had embraced the full course on offer at Silverton and had jumped that hurdle with total dedication. What we didn't realise at the time were the lengths to which that course would go. Am I giving away trade secrets? Well, no. The events chronicled here took place some years ago and, as you have probably guessed, Dear Reader, names, addresses, even counties have been substituted, so if it amuses you to go for a spin down Dartmoor way, I can only wish you well and hope the weather stays fine for you. You will be careful on the moors though, won't you; those marshy areas are very treacherous.

25014710R00068

Printed in Poland
by Amazon Fulfillment
Poland Sp. z o.o., Wrocław